Rhythm of the Sea

2nd Edition

Revised and Expanded

Shari Cohen

www.beachhousebooks.com

BeachHouse Books is an Imprint of

Science & Humanities Press

Saint Charles, MO 63301

Copyright

Graphics Credits:

Foreword and Cover by Dr. Bud Banis. The front cover is based on an original photograph by Shari Cohen.

Publication date September, 2021

ISBN 978-1-59630-115-3   BeachHouse Books Edition

ISBN 978-1-59630-116-0   MacroPrintBooks Edition

First Printing, September, 2021

Library of Congress Cataloging-in-Publication Data of the first edition:
Cohen, Shari.
 Rhythm of the Sea / Shari Cohen.
   p.cm.
 ISBN 1-888725-55-9 (alk. paper)
1. United States--Social life and customs--20th century--Fiction. I. Title.
PS3553.O4276 R48 2001
813'.54--dc21
                        2001003187

www.beachhousebooks.com

BeachHouse Books an Imprint of

Science & Humanities Press

Saint Charles, MO 63301

TO PAUL

A million more sunsets

Foreword

Twenty years.

A new generation. And a new edition of this book, reflecting evolutionary changes with time. Sand castles and lines written in the sand are continually renewed and silently washed away with the impassive tides.

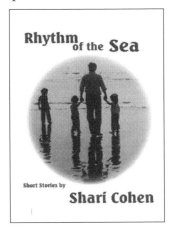 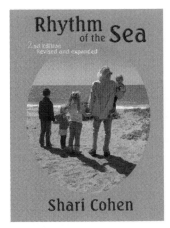

This book is about relationships. The stories are delightfully diverse, but have a common thread in that each is set in a background related to a body of water.

Water has an almost universal appeal. Most people are relaxed by the sounds of waves, a brook, a gentle rain, the roar of a giant waterfall, even the passing of a thunderstorm. These sounds, and the images that go with them, have an almost magical calming effect, allowing our minds to float free and feel a sense of harmony with nature and the world around us.

The rhythm of moving water creates a mood for contemplation allowing us to put things together and understand ourselves better free of the distractions of everyday life.

It's ironic that introspection is often the key to understanding other people. We infer that others around us have the same feelings and needs—know the same sorrows and pains—by observing their behavior and comparing their feelings to our own. Only by understanding ourselves do we know what other people are going through.

Reading is another way to discover meaning and relate to what other people are thinking and feeling. Shari Cohen's short stories in Rhythm of the Sea are that kind of reading.

Think of how these stories could relate to you:

In Clear as a Belle, an ignored old woman is heard only through the unassuming ears of her grandchildren. Adults assume she lives only in her irrelevant own mind.

Lost in the Fog, a young man finds an unexpected connection during a lunchtime dalliance on the beach. A tempting, but brief potential new relationship.

In The Gift, after years of wondering, a 40-year-old married woman returns to the Oregon Coast hoping to see her first love again. What she experiences may be something that you have known.

In Rightful Journey, a father runs out to sea because he has difficulty dealing with his son's disability, and learns a lesson from the seas.

In The Goodbye Place, a teen from a small Midwest town yearns to run away to the west coast to be a rock star. At his favorite pond area, he has a vision which gives him new insight on his strengths.

In Lifeline, a young boy seeks respect from the bullies in a small town, and finds a common bond with the worst of them all.

In Alien Heart, two come to earth from a distant galaxy as advance spies to facilitate the plunder of Earth's water-rich resources, but the mission takes an unexpected turn.

In Eyes of the Gull, an old widow living in a nursing home seeks the soul of her husband.

In The Rhythm of Life, we realize that what we sometimes see as duty can become a reward, as an old man who wanted to sail the waters alone all his life recounts and realizes what it was that kept him home.

Finally, we find a Rhythm of the Soul, which supersedes other attractions to bring Dr. David Chen back to his care for young patients — the real meaning in his life.

This brief foreword only gives a hint of the breadth of the stories, but every one of them relates to some common experience.

In reading Shari's stories, you will recognize yourself, and when you do, you will have a new view of yourself and how you relate to other people. You will be touched by Shari's stories about other living beings, and you will think about how much we share.

One person's life may seem only a brief moment in the millions of years of human history, but the ripples that we leave behind began with some person far in the past and continue on into the future. We each affect each other, like ripples in a pond or waves in an ocean. In this way, we each affect eternity.

We are not alone.

An ocean runs through us all and we live our lives together in the Rhythm of the Sea.

Robert J. Banis, PhD
St. Louis, Missouri
August, 2021

"The sea, once it casts its spell,

holds one in its net of wonder forever."

— *Jacques Cousteau*

Stories

Clear as a Belle

Eighty-year-old Belle Barton sat stone still on the weathered bench atop a seaweed- strewn knoll facing the Pacific. Belle's bench, here long before the Northern California Memory Care Facility where she now resided, was her only touchstone beyond the facility. Fittingly secure on the miniscule strand of beach fifty yards down from the institute's outdoor patio/cabana, the bench's white paint chipped and peeling, weather-beaten, seemed that much more invincible, in its aged, diminished form. How much longer she would be allowed to come down to this bench unaccompanied remained to be seen.

Belle was officially diagnosed a year earlier with Alzheimer's disease by a specialist, and by her daughter Jean and son-in-law, Mark months before that. Mark, a CPA, suspected her mind was slipping and would burden her day with small memory tests to take, such as a cousin or family member's name to see if she recalled them. Jean and Mark had apparently not factored in her disinterest in said distant cousins when she did not work very hard for the right answer. It did not take long before personal tragedy, age, and forgetfulness morphed into slow, mental decline. And they took her in for a more authoritative verdict.

This development had capped two years of turmoil and loneliness after Belle's husband Milt had passed away from a sudden stoke. After the protracted bereavement, her beloved home became the issue. She loved the tiny rural home they lived in and refused to leave, over the many requests of her family: "No apartment, but thank you," she told her daughter Jean, again and again. "Guest house, Mark? I don't think so." She especially didn't want to move in with them. "I do appreciate the offer," she answered again and again.

Though she had to adjust to the new reality, her wants were defined. She filled her days with gardening, needlepoint, and baking cookies and treats for her three grandchildren. She watched old movies on the oldies network that played them day and night. And her home was a gallery to her beloved Milt who looked out at her in photos from every wall and mantel throughout the house. The walls reverberated at odd moments with his gravelly voice of adoration. Milt's caring spirit and lifetime of memories imprinted in her heart. In that home, Love was with her always

It didn't last. As time passed, the memories in Belle's heart yearned for Milt's real presence, tangible offerings of love and comfort. It was then she ached for him.

Belle and Milt had a strong and beautiful relationship, their respect for one another its lifeblood. She especially missed Milt during the holidays. At Halloween, their favorite, the outside of their home became a Disneyland of ghouls for those driving by below. Pumpkins lined the walkway. Cut-out characters she had purchased from a nearby craft store were placed facing different ways for all to see. Her pumpkin pies, topped with swirls of whipped cream were a favorite with family and nearby neighbors, who had become like family over the years.

At the end of that two-year period after Milt passed, memories were not working anymore, they began to shred and disappear. The strongest memories of her life with Milt held her together, but only for so long.

In their place, over time, depression insinuated itself during the following weeks and months. She stopped baking. Old movies made her cry uncontrollably. She drew all the curtains in her house and evaded bright colors. She filtered out all sounds of the neighborhood kids. All color drained from her life, inside the home and out, all fading to gray that had no spark or meaning. The sun setting over the rocky buffs in the distance, in all its orange and fiery red glory went unnoticed. Even the sights and sounds of an approaching late summer storm was just that- an approaching storm. She and Milt use to stand by their enormous front window and watch the trees whip wildly in the wind. Milt would announce the gathering black clouds amassing power, inching closer, then exploding with sounds of rumbling thunder and strikes of bright lightening. They especially enjoyed the evening storms, when they would fall asleep under the steady rhythm of the rain from the rooftop overhead.

Now, the storms had no power over Belle whose grief was turning toxic inside. Jean noticed the change in many ways, particularly at Belle's favorite restaurant – Danny's Diner. Jean and Mark enjoyed taking Belle to the 50's place not far from Belle's home. The conversation always was about the delicious food brought to their table. Mark laughed as Belle struggled with her oversized burger and imprinted a moustache from her favorite vanilla shake. She swayed to the tunes that played around them, smiling and closing her eyes, taking it all in. But after Milt left them, those times began disappearing as well. Jean and Mark were saddened, as they now would be the ones leading the conversations. Belle sat quietly, picking at her food, then pushing the plate away. Soon, their visits to Danny's Diner became less and less, then ceased.

Belle was eventually taken to a senior portion of a nearby hospital and given cognitive tests to determine her mental stamina. What plans would have to put into action, her daughter wondered. Belle's memory was tested. Rachel, the doctor's assistant, placed exam papers in front of her. Words, numbers, basic situations were explained and then asked what she would do in each case. She sat stone-faced, looking down at the papers in front of her. She did not care how she scored. For what purpose did she have to add 4 + 8? Belle's mind retreated to that private grotto presided over by her beloved Milt, safely out of touch and insulated by memories of the two of them, hugging, laughing, making plans to decorate their home for Christmas. She handed the exam papers back to Rachel, crossing her arms and staring at the wall.

And so, it was decided that the best place for Belle was at the nearby Memory Care facility. Jean thought her mother would fight her in this decision. But she went quietly.

Belle settled into her new life at the facility. Jean set up family photos on her mother's nightstand. Her clothes were neatly folded in drawers and placed on hangers in the closet.

"Do you like it?" Jean asked her, pointing to the large window and table below lined with vases of fresh purple and yellow flowers. She received a fleeting smile.

Weeks passed without incident. The staff, Jean and Mark made sure Belle was being taken care of. Update calls were made back and forth. Belle became a bit of a celebrity: she was the only resident in the small facility that would daily venture out of doors, down to the private beach. The bench became hers. No one bothered her. She would sit motionless for hours sometimes, but it was evident to her keepers that the perch by the water was fulfilling a need.

In time it became routine for the grandchildren to visit their Granny Belle twice a month on Saturdays. Simon, now 11, Lexie, 9- and 6-year-old Frankie ran to the bench to hug her and took their usual places. Simon to the left, Lexie on the right and Frankie usually jumping on the sand in front of her. Better than any medication, Belle thought, as she embraced each of them. They were like oxygen to her. They breathed life into her aging body. Their laughter made her spirits soar. Frankie's funny faces- his spontaneous hugs filled her heart with joy. Each child brought light and hope to Belle.

The children were a blessing, in contrast to the staff in the Memory Center, who looked at her as if she were invisible. She received quick smiles, but little eye contact. The only conversation was between the staff members themselves, the helpers and assistants, who spoke to each other while tending to her needs. They were kind and polite, but there was no real direct communication with Belle. She knew that in their minds, they felt she would not understand what was being said. She would not find humor in a funny joke. She would not appreciate the sweet taste of a new dessert offered. The stigma to what she was diagnosed, was standard in the care of the facility. When families visited, they would see their loved ones were being cared for. They were in clean clothes, given three meals a day and correct medications were handed out to those who required them. In Belle's case, her daughter Jean realized there were no more back and forth discussions with her mother of politics.

There was no asking of her opinion on how a new pair of shoes looked on her. Gone were the moments of shared daily experiences and humor.

At odd moments it was evident to anyone looking closely that Belle's inner flame still burned bright. Her inner senses were acute and aware, her feelings strong and steadfast. Anger, joy, fear are not emotions so easily dismissed...all were working within her. But all these life-affirming attributes were not on display for everyone. To anyone in the facility looking downward to the bench where Belle was hemmed in by her grandkids it was obvious that Belle's inner flame was reflected in the hearts and minds of these three young believers. It was the wonder in their eyes- their giggles-professing their love for her that was the force bringing her back to life.

At the ocean's edge, with the loves of her life hovering, Belle felt young and strong. She delighted in talking about the time she was growing up in the 1950's, in a town outside of San Francisco.

"1950's? When was that?" Simon asked.

"Did they have cell phones?" Lexie asked.

"No," Belle answered. "No cell phones. Our phone was a black square, sitting on a table with a cord reaching to a handle. To speak with someone on the phone you dialed each number on a dial pad. Clickety-Clickety- Clickety- Click," she laughed.

Memories of her younger years intrigued them. She told them about the time she met their grandfather Milt when they were teenagers. "Love at first sight," she sighed. "For both of us. We loved going to movies and roller skating at the Metro Palace Center." She closed her eyes describing the dimly lit room with blinking blue lights on the walls.

She told them about their favorite candy treats of the past. Baby Ruth Candy Bars...with the sweetest taste of peanuts, chocolate and caramel. Big Hunk, Bonamo's Turkish Taffy, Necco Wafers.

Simon held out his had to her. "Wish I had one now," he teased.

Every visit the children would watch their grandmother spellbound, feeling so privileged to be the only witness to her beachside revival: her wrinkled animated face, her eyes now widening as she told them about the flat chunks of Taffy- the slow melting pieces could last for hours. And everyone's favorite back then- Bazooka Bubblegum and PEZ cherry candy, wrapped in a long red container with the blue and white letters P E Z displayed in white squares.

Month after month, the children learned something new about their Granny Belle. She talked about her favorite music from that time- the singing groups she enjoyed.

"Buddy Holly was my favorite," she told them. Buddy Holly and the Crickets. When she sang she remembered all the words: "It's so easy to fall in love...It's so easy to fall in love", she crooned.

The children smiled watching Granny Belle sway and bop to the catchy tune.

"You know, Elvis was the King!" She reminded them. "The King of Rock and Roll. You ain't nothing but a Hound Dog, crying all the time," she chided Frankie, who began laughing.

Every other Saturday afternoon, Belle entertained her grandchildren down on the strand on what had become her private beach preserve while her daughter and son-in-law watched with their lattes from the patio above and discussed "serious matters" with the weekend doctor, sitting with other families there to visit. Looking down at the white bench, Jean watched her kids dance and sing in front of her mother.

"I don't know how they can give her so much attention in the shape she is in, but I'm so grateful," she told the doctor, as they watched the children performing, laughing and hugging her. Their energy seemed to know no bounds.

Others on the patio looked at the three kids barefoot in the sand, watching the children singing tunes- their voices disappearing into the ocean air. "How sweet your children are," they often commented to Jean. "Yes," another agreed. "It is wonderful to see the time and attention they give your mother."

While those who were gathered on the upper patio behind her talked and had coffee and snacks, Belle's spirit was dancing with the young ones before her. She knew the words to so many songs from her past and sang them with amusing facial expressions. The three children learned the songs and sang with her, jumping off the bench to play a make-believe guitar, a keyboard and dance haphazardly in the sand.

"I'm Chuck Berry!" Frankie shouted. "See me Reelin and a Rockin'?"

"Till the break of dawn!" Simon chimed in.

"Lexi?" Simon pointed to her-

"You mean Elvis?" She grinned. "One for the money, two for the show, three to get ready…. Now go Cat go"…

As the months passed, Belle's apprentice musicians learned more tunes from their Granny Belle.

"Hi Lexi," Belle greeted her granddaughter on a cloudy Saturday afternoon visit.

"No, Granny- I'm Doris Day, "she squealed. She held out her arms and sang in tune, twirling about in the salty ocean air- "Que sera, sera, whatever will be, will be… The future's not ours to see, Que sera, sera"..

"What will be, will be…." Belle shrieked in delight.

Lexi ran into her arms and was swallowed in a giant hug. A single tear ran down the right side of elderly woman's face. When she cried, Belle always had one tear that took it's time on its way down. Milt often teased her about it.

"A single tear? Where are the others?" he wanted to know.

The young girl looked up and saw her granny swipe at the lone tear, brushing it aside where it disappeared into the damp wind.

The 80-year old's mind was like an ongoing movie. Colorful stories, so long buried, were now bursting upon a screen. It was almost as if Belle was living back in the 50's as a teenager, experiencing life in the moment. It was a life in suburbs, with drive-in movies, TV dinners, hula hoops and Saddle Shoes.

What Belle loved was that her grandchildren did not roll their eyes and laugh when she reminisced. They wanted details. They wanted to know more.

Once, six-year-old Frankie tried to tell his parents some of the things Granny Belle talked about and that she sang the words to old songs. But Simon put his hand on his brother's shoulder with a hard tweak. It didn't matter: Jean rolled her eyes and his dad laughed.

"Frankie," he said. "We've had this talk. Your grandmother does not sing songs. She does not remember lyrics or much of anything, these days. She barely recognizes us, but we know that she loves you. And we are so happy you are spending time with her."

Behind their back all three kids smiled and nodded.

October arrived with a chill. Grey clouds hovered during the weeks over the Northern California coast. People walking near the shore were bundled up in sweaters and jackets. A light fog carried in it, mist that looked like it would soon become droplets of rain. The first notice that something might be wrong with their grandmother was when Simon and Frankie arrived at the white bench ahead of Lexi. She acknowledged them, but not with her usual hugs. She appeared quiet and when Lexi arrived, she saw her grandmother talking, then stopping to catch her breath.

With the damp weather increasing, the staff huddled and decided to go down early to bring her back inside. With some alarm, they noticed she was unsteady on her feet. Walking was an effort. They motioned to the patio for a wheelchair to be brought down. Her family saw the decline in energy and plans were made for her to see a physician in the morning.

Jean woke the grandchildren early the next morning with devastating news. Their granny did not make it through the night. Her heart, they were told, failed. "She did not suffer," Jean assured them. "Her heart went into a final sleep- peacefully in the late hours, as did she."

Jean and Mark gathered the children into their arms. No more words were spoken. Each was lost in her own thoughts about the finality of what happened.

Later, Jean told each child how proud she was of them. "You gave her your time and your love."

The following day, the staff and Belle's family gathered into a reception room at Memory Care to pay their respects. A long table bisected the middle. They stood in a circle around the table, commenting on framed photos of Belle with Milt, Jean and Mark, and the grandchildren. Jean was the first to speak. She talked about her mother and how much she will be missed. She shared a few stories with the staff, about her mother's favorite times with the family- Cooking and baking for them, decorating for the holidays. Mark spoke about Danny's Diner where his mother-in law ate burgers, fries and shakes, while moving to the music to the delight of others around her. Many of the staff had nice things to say.

"She was patient, never caused trouble, a sweet and kind lady", they agreed.

The room became quiet. They looked at Simon and Lexi, and Frankie who stood between them. And at that moment, the children began to talk about their beloved grandmother. They spoke about her life growing up in Santa Rosa in the 1950's. They shared her favorite foods to eat, her favorite sweet treats... her love of drive in movies, about meeting their grandfather Milt for the first time and their dates at the Metro Palace Skating Center. As they spoke, Jean and Mark looked at each other with complete surprise.

"How do you know this?" their mother asked. "How would you know what her life was like back in her time?"

"We know"… Frankie answered. "We know the music she liked, Lexi chimed in. Buddy Holly, Chuck Berry-

"Don't forget Elvis!" Simon added.

"And Doris Day," Lexi reminded.

"We know she did not like eggs every day for breakfast," Simon blushed, telling the staff." She loved blueberry pancakes, like the ones you had made for yourselves."

"She said she wore brightly colored wool skirts with a wide belt and bobby socks," Lexi told them. "And she had a black phone that sat on a table- that you had to use your finger to dial each number- Clickety- Clickety- Clickety- Click!" Frankie giggled.

Through her grandchildren, Belle Barton's memories were shared, as real when talking about them as they were when she experienced them so many years ago. Sounds, sights, feelings exploded into reality. Nothing was imagined. Everything- real. The children welcomed this era, when so much was different. It did not feel odd or strange. They could feel what she felt. Her spirit that had been floundering in a cloud of grey had burst open with new life and crystal-clear images. The children captured her raw emotion, her humor, her honesty and held on to it. They would treasure the time they spent with her and although they did not know it now, they would have amazing stories to tell to their future families, as they grew older and had children of their own.

After the gathering, Jean, Mark and the kids went out to the back patio. "I want to say goodbye to the friends we made here," Jean told the kids.

Lexi looked down at the empty bench facing the sea.

"I'm going down there- I will be right back," she announced. She left her brothers with her parents and ran across the sand. Sitting in the middle of the bench, Lexi closed her eyes.

A lone tear ran down the right side of her face. She brushed it away, where it disappeared into the misty afternoon breeze. "I know you are going back to the time you loved most," she whispered. "You will be with your friends and with grandpa... young, happy and well."

Then she looked up and with her hand, blew a kiss to the clouds.

"Sleep with the angels Granny Belle."

Lost in the Fog

Stealing a glance at the ocean out of the conference room's immense bay window, Derek Williams thought the sky strange somehow before turning back to take his place at the shiny oak table and meticulously arranged paperwork in front of him. Friday's weekly case review. Routine. For the next five minutes, in between sips of his strong Columbian coffee, he made the usual small talk with his associates before again looking out to sea to the distant fog bank that seemed in his mind's eye to be inching forward by the moment. Indeed, as the meeting droned on, the fog bank's progress seemed more pronounced and menacing, a thick grey rampart eclipsing both sunlight and the September sky. Yet no one else seemed to notice as they chattered amongst themselves taking turns spouting their time worn legal opinions.

Derek did his due diligence, chiming in here and there, offering his thoughts to his colleagues, then asking for their reviews on his current caseload. His fellow senior partners held the fifty-year-old's opinions in high regard. After eighteen years at the firm, Derek's almost stereotypic "tall, dark and handsome" sculpted looks had little altered, save a few haphazard streaks of grey in his shoulder-length dark hair. Likewise, his magnetic presence still resonated, tempered by his sense of humor and endearing smile, in both client and colleague.

His blessings did not end at the firm. The lawyer was a devoted husband to his wife Maggie and Dad to fourteen-year-old twin boys Sam and Daniel, who adored him. He and Maggie, best friends and confidents, shared a quirky sense of humor and both had a strict, but easy and loving manner with their two boys. Together they worked hard raising their sons in the California city of Santa Monica. Maggie worked as a teacher at a school in Los Angeles and Derek spent his days at the law firm he founded with three other associates almost two decades before in an older brick building near the ocean. The law firm had burgeoned to a dozen talented and respectable attorneys who took great pride in their work. Over time, his crew of co-workers and their families became personal friends.

Derek looked at this watch and yawned. It had been two hours and the meeting had ended. He was back in his office making calls to clients.

At lunchtime, he grabbed his briefcase, took the elevator to the main floor and walked out to pick up his usual sandwich at the bagel shop next door. Derek hated eating his lunch inside restaurants in the area. The hour he spent left him open to walking out on the sand and eating at one of several tattered wooden picnic tables that were secured where the sidewalk met the sand.

There he sat, in black jeans and a tan leather sports jacket, wearing sunglasses, working on files, while watching the troupe of people going about their business. Some were perched at tables, working under the warmth of the afternoon sun eating their lunch, others skirting the water's edge, watching the waves hammering the shoreline — retreating and then crawling closer each time as if in a rhythmic dance. These faces that walked and ran about the ocean's edge appeared calmer to Derek, not stressed like some that worked in offices along the way.

Today, as every day, seabirds hovered above, a few dropping down to greet him, his longtime friends. They did not flinch when he reached out close, to toss a piece of bread their way. Derek felt he could pet them and they would stay. He was familiar with the seagull's jerky movements of their heads and small round eyes that stared, waiting for the next bite of food. Derek knew their rituals. Once, when he was laid up at home from a broken ankle, he was unable to make his daily rendezvous with his feathered friends for almost two weeks.

When he returned, they squawked their greetings as if welcoming him back. Were their squawks that much louder, he smiled? So much more animated? Of course, he was probably imagining it...but it amused him immensely.

"Hello," he saluted them as he tossed out a piece of his sandwich to them.

The closest one grabbed it, holding tight in its long orange beak. Shredding a bite, the bird turned around and tossed it to the one behind. The second one nibbled from the jagged piece and turned to share it with a third behind him.

When the gulls were done, they flew as a group out to the giant rocky bluff off-shore. There, they yelled out in their own language their thoughts and comments for the day. Derek heard their squawks, cackles and screeches- high and low tones, as if they were answering each other in a friendship gathering. Some flew outward towards the deeper part of the sea. Others flew a straight line and returned to the jagged mountain ledges moments later. What a grand life they have, Derek thought. Walking, talking, feeding and visiting out around the waters- feelings so familiar in their pattern of life - deliberate and unwavering.

Derek checked his watch. He looked up and watched the gulls who strode in front of him, some landing on empty picnic tables, others sharing littered food on the sand, flying back and forth in the distance. Then, oddly he had to blink twice to clear his vision. The gulls were there but blurred by a light haze. The fog bank he had noticed earlier, had advanced to the shore. Now, it was hovering and settling downward, over him. Derek stood and tossed his soda cup and sandwich remains in a garbage container a few feet away.

Then he grabbed his briefcase and walked away from his table, looking upward. The sky was gone. It had disappeared in the low thick cloud that hovered and surrounded him.

Strange, he thought. I'm not sure which way to turn to get back to the building.

He began walking in the direction he thought was correct. But there was no way of knowing exactly where he had wandered. I'm really and truly lost in the fog, he chuckled, albeit nervously. It was not that funny. He felt trapped. A creeping feeling of anxiety rose within him. There were no distinct voices calling out, only a few echoes with high and low tones, mumbling in the distance. There were no car motors running, horns honking or tires screeching as they usually did when they backed up from the nearby building's parking lot.

From a distance, he did hear a muted crash upon the shore that rang familiar. Waves, he knew, making their presence known with an arrival splash — then pulling back, stalling and hammering the shore again and again in familiar repeated intervals.

Derek walked blindly in different directions. His legs were getting tired. His shoes were filling with sand, his feet feeling awkward and uneven with each forward step. This can't last forever, he spoke to the mist, whose blanket of grey wet air, hindered and dull held him captive. Taking off his sport jacket, Derek used it as a small blanket and placed it on the sand. He took off his shoes, shook out the sand and sat down.

The mist felt damp on his face and he shivered. The fog was all encompassing; there were no clear openings to see through.

He reached for his phone, hopeful, before reminding himself there was never cell service out on the beach. His phone would not start working until he reached the sidewalk, where all the office buildings and businesses were aligned.

Suddenly from his right side, a figure appeared. A woman. Visible. Distinct. He jumped when she crowded abruptly into his now claustrophobic space.

"Oh, sorry", she exclaimed nervously when she peered downward and saw the handsome man sitting on top of his jacket.

Derek looked up at the woman as if through a mysterious curtain. Very pretty, early 40s, he noted as she pushed long dark bangs away from hazel eyes, nervously catching and holding his gaze, then smiling as she clutched at a notebook and adjusted an enormous purse slipping off her shoulder. She was fashionably dressed in a dark blue suede blazer and jeans, wearing a silver necklace and matching hooped earrings. Then he looked down at her shoes — designer he was sure — but like his own, they were filled with damp pebbles and chunks of sand. He chuckled.

"Have a seat", he offered, patting the sand next to him. "Don't know how long this will last, but it beats wandering around in circles."

She sat delicately, then looked at him. "I'm Jade," she said, emptying her shoes. He held out his hand and she shook it awkwardly. "I was working down the way and decided to take a stroll", she told him. "But the strangest thing started happening"…..

"You don't have to tell me", he laughed.

"I thought I knew every inch of this beach. I work not far from here- or back there… or is it over there" he pointed jokingly. "This is the first time I've ever lost my bearings on a simple work, day minutes from my office."

He watched her study him for a moment, suddenly feeling self-conscious about his wedding band.

"At least we landed in a safe space," she kidded. "We're not stuck in an elevator."

"Agreed," Derek responded, feeling more relaxed, despite the inexplicable moments of awkwardness. As the momentary self-consciousness dissolved, the words came tumbling out, both talking at once. Their words spilled forth, questions flying from Jade, then Derek. What was Derek's favorite football team? What kind of music did he like...country? Rock? Classics? Hearing his answers, she confided her obsessions- for reggae music, for comfort foods- pizzas, burgers, fries and ice cream. He smiled and reveled in her talk, in her voice, low, whispery, musical — flowing upward in lilting crescendo.

Derek was transfixed, intrigued by the woman beside him. Strangers no more, they talked like reunited lifelong friends, protected in some sort of foggy cocoon. Yet each was aware that the low-lying cloud would soon open and they would be re-released back into the real world.

Derek looked at her again. It could have been worse, he smiled to himself. He could be sitting next to someone who did not want to speak. Someone who had an attitude, with a sharp tone or sarcasm in response to his small talk.

He imagined his friend Tony, the recently divorced co-worker who had eyes for every good-looking female that crossed his path. After greetings and small talk, Tony would have asked for Jade's number. He would have made plans to see her again and the inches between them on the sand would become smaller as he would pull himself close.

Derek's briefcase lay on its side away from him. The first time he could remember not having it within direct reach. Jade's purse and notebook sat half buried in the sand. There was no great desire to grab these items. They talked politics, and about their love for movies.

"Horror flicks," Jade confided, looking at him- waiting for him to roll his eyes in ridicule. "My favorite."

"Me, too," Derek admitted. "I like the old ones from the 50's in black and white."

Time stood still as they talked and laughed and connected. Neither seemed to want this experience to end.

Jade told him she was here on a one-time visit and would be leaving soon. What she did not share was that she had no one to return to. She was recently divorced from a man who she discovered had a heart of stone. In earlier years, she used to laugh openly had many friends and embraced life. Over time this man tried to keep her quiet, to talk for her, to make himself the center of attention. With coldness and persistence, he had won. He had stolen her spirit. He had stolen her light. She was relieved when the last separation documents were signed, but now she was truly alone.

By the end of this day Jade would be on an airplane where a taxi would be waiting at the other end, taking her to her apartment in a desert town outside of Phoenix. She had always loved the desert — the vast openness and picturesque mountains.
But Jade loved the ocean more. She had been to the west coast a few times in her life. She always remembered the feeling of awe, seeing fishing boats gathering at night, each lit up in different colors breaking through the darkness like an array of Christmas lights. There were times she would stop in her tracks when walking along the shore and stare out at yellow-orange sunsets inching downward at the end of the day to make way for the moon's grand entrance. Sometimes it was a full moon, sometimes a sliver, its glow rising to light up the night sky. How lucky to be able to live near the sea. And now, she was completing her services as an interior home designer for a client. When the fog lifted, she would be on her way, back home where she would continue working, usually in the cities around Phoenix. Unless....

She glanced at Derek. He had closed his eyes, listening to the sea water slam the shore somewhere in the distance when…he felt her hand touch his. She kept it there, over his, until instinctively he pulled his back. He straightened up a bit, brushing off sand from his pants. It was as if he lowered an invisible screen between them. Talking, laughing, sharing life's moments with a stranger under these circumstances seemed natural. After all, it would not be much longer when the two would part and each would walk away, in their own direction.

But accepting a touch from another woman brought forth a strange response in Derek. And now, the more he inched to the side, the closer Jade slid towards him.

He thought of his wife. Maggie is the one who should have been there. She would laugh at their situation but be captivated by the moment. He would hold her in his arms, and they would add this to the many off-beat predicaments they often found themselves in. She would be worrying about the children, the housework, making dinner… Yet during these moments her eyes would stay on her husband. Derek knew the love his wife carried for himself and their family. For years in the future, she would bring up … do you remember the time?

But Maggie was not beside him. This was Jade- a serious but fun-loving beauty who had been slowly breaking his heart. In a subtle way she was trying to show him what could be. He knew if he relented, if he showed a spark of wanting, of interest even in a kidding way– there would be no turning back. His strong will could betray him and act on its own…exposing weakness…knowing wrong from right but not caring.

The murky mist enveloping them seemed to lighten. This caused them to look at one another as if realizing they would no longer be captive inside the air cloud. His hand reached across the sand and pulled his briefcase close, next to his side.

If he asked, she would stay. Jade knew she would be available, whenever, wherever he wanted her. She imagined them inseparable, walking along streets filled with shops, laughing, stopping to buy treats in the bakeries, exploring life together. They would live in a state of adoration and fantasy.

She looked at Derek again, then down at the gold ring on his left hand. Jade knew it was the reason she may never have a chance.

Derek cleared his throat and looked at his watch.

The fog cleared, exposing movement and color. The two stood, brushing sand off themselves. It was time to walk away, to pull themselves together and continue on in their day.

When he glanced away for a moment, Jade reached down and placed her card on his briefcase. In full view, it had her picture, along with various ways to contact her through email, text and her business website. In her mind, she had given him the key, for without this card, there would be no way to reach her. The two had not given each other specifics- such as information about where they lived. They spoke of politics, of favorite foods and movies but did not share their last names or anything personal in that time capsule.

It would be up to Derek to call her if he wanted, Jade realized. She hoped one day in the future, when this meeting was still fresh in his mind, she might hear from him. Perhaps if times changed, if things began to fade in his marriage…if his desire for someone new overtook his feelings…how, when, why she didn't know. She would always remember this man who touched her soul.

They hugged each other tightly. Jade walked away. As he turned to pick up his briefcase, and unbeknownst to Derek, a seagull swooped down and grabbed Jade's card with direct aim. Other gulls waddled in closer. The first gull nibbled at the card, shredding it. The gull turned and tossed it to his friend behind him, who pecked at it, dropped it and let the third gull have the remaining torn piece. They took the last bit of card and flew out to their mountain landing on the water, passing it back and forth among them. There, it was tossed out into a high swirling gust of wind, where it eventually dropped and was carried out to sea.

Into the churning waters it disappeared, carrying with it the rightful key....defining honor — commitment - and everlasting love.

The Gift

"Welcome home," Anne muttered to herself and saluted as she turned onto the coast highway in the van she rented just hours earlier at the airport.

She thought about the tone of her simple salutation. Anxious, apprehensive, admonishing as if to a child, she wondered? No, not the latter. She was not a child, but a forty-year-old woman, a wife and mother. But was she acting like one, she smiled, when her true home was back in Boston? Perhaps she should be there now in these days before Christmas–wrapping gifts and making plans for the holiday.

But she was here thousands of miles away for only one reason: to see Sam.

It had been over twenty years since she and Sam Banks said their goodbyes. She said his name aloud. It sounded so strange, this name from the past, this name that would not let her rest. The sound of his murmured name reminded her of its quiet and constant iteration...over and over in her head...for so many years.

How many more years could she have gone on masquerading the feelings this name invoked?

When her husband Frank asked her what she wanted most for Christmas this year, she spoke the words without thinking, the words held back for so long. "I want to go home for just a day." The home to which she alluded was on another coast, a gorgeous coast, a place far removed from her present home in the big city. It was a rugged and desolate region of land.

She waited for Frank's puzzled face, his raised eyebrow, a gentle reprimand. It never came. A few days later he handed her a ticket, wrapped in a red bow. With a hug, he said, "Go, and do what you must. I'll be here and take charge."

As she drove down the coast of the semi-deserted December highway in the drizzle, she had second thoughts. She should've changed her mind right then and stayed, she thought, and the three of them — Frank and Anne and their daughter — would be listening to Christmas music, wrapping the last of the presents, and toying with the final decorations on the tree. She blinked her eyes briefly and saw her family now without her, gathered near the cozy warmth of the fire, in the dim and festive-glowed living room, the colored lights strung haphazardly about the walls. She saw her daughter Jenny's face beaming, eyes aglow with eagerness and exhilaration.

Instead, Anne was miles away on another coast, staring out at hundreds of seabirds riding the thermal air currents high over the rocky cliffs of the Northwest. Falling, rising, floating, she watched them, spellbound, as they spread their wings to full capacity and played, suspending themselves in mid-air, not able to make any forward momentum.

Just as she was at this very moment, playing in time and space.

Anne slowed and leaned to peer up at the seabirds through the front window of the van. She turned off the road and parked, then closed her eyes and clutched the wheel for a long minute or two.

Stepping out, she walked up a winding pathway that led to the windblown grassy bluff out toward the headland. Once there, she surveyed the majesty of the scene before her. Below were more birds, thousands, like white raindrops swirling over the once-familiar picture-postcard sand drifts and dunes which rippled and stretched for miles, fronting the adjacent thick timberland peninsula.

After more than two decades she was back at this most rugged section of the Oregon Coast. It greeted her like an old friend, primping and boasting its subdued grandiosity, as if to remind her of all that she had missed. And Anne saw its powerful beauty like she never had before.

Anne felt her senses besieged. In the mist the salt air was suddenly swept with the sweet aroma of fragrant blossoms. Her eyes dallied over the pink and purple wild flowers and deep rooted shrubs and bushes that led the way up to the highest bluffs, jutting out over a wild and churning sea. As if on cue, she heard and saw in her mind's eye the herds of sea lions and their pups carousing on the rocks in the grotto below. Anne smiled and closed her eyes, seeing them frolic in the splashes of wild ocean as it surged in and out of the caves.

Suddenly hedging, she started to turn and walk back to her car. Then in mid- motion she stopped and once again looked out to the sea. How far should she take it? There was still time to turn around and take the evening flight back. But the flame so long flickering was burning bright. There had never been any way to put it out. Especially now.

Year after year it smoldered, haunting her with what if? What if she had stayed behind and made a life here with Sam? Would she be happy now? Or peaceful with her lot in womanhood. Or would her heart nag still, restless and agitated, as in her youth when her heart drove her away?

Anne left Sam in that youth, right after high school, a dauntless, self-assured young woman with stars in her eyes, college-bound with scholarship in hand. She promised Sam she'd return from Boston a fully-degreed teacher. Sam's sadness showed, she supposed he knew he might never see her again. His face also showed he fully understood his destiny to stay behind: the eldest, he was chosen to carry on in the family business.

How quickly the two decades passed. And how quickly the strangeness overtook her former optimism now that she was just minutes from seeing him again. Anne knew he was divorced and had a teenage son for whom he retained custody and was raising in the same beach house where he grew up at North Point.

She recalled her hands shaking the day she was alone at home and phoned him to announce her visit. His voice broke when he first heard hers and for a few moments the two spoke awkwardly, stumbling over their words.

Anne listened as he talked, feeling almost a shared pride in his son, Michael. "A great kid. Solid. Strong with values and a good heart," Sam told her. "I've always wanted you to meet him."

She closed her eyes as he spoke, hearing his voice, this wraith from the past. He sounded different and she wondered how he looked after all these years. Did he think of her, she wondered? Did he remember the whimsical times they shared, walking hand-in-hand along secret pathways—running, playing ball, picnicking and sharing secrets and ambitions along the miles of isolated beaches?

Guilt stabbed at her briefly when she thought of her kind and thoughtful husband, Frank, a man she loved. He was a successful young attorney who had courted her while Anne was a student at the university in Boston. They married soon after Anne graduated. After waiting ten years, they had their only child, a daughter named Jenny.

At first, when Frank proposed, she thought of Sam waiting for her back on the coast and the promise she made to return. But by then he was so far removed from what she was and was to become since leaving North Point. Anne was moving up at a fast furious pace.

Sam called each day to ask when she was coming home. She resented his voice grown increasingly colorless, as she made her empty assurances. The calls ceased. At that time, Sam was a boy compared to her intended, the teen-aged vows made on a bluff overlooking the Pacific, immature and frivolous and naive. Not as serious as her new life, nor marriage.

After graduation, Anne began teaching second grade. She and Frank thrived in the community with good careers and friends. So happy were they that Anne vowed to coax her parents into following, no matter how long it took. Eventually they did and settled in a small town outside of Boston. Anne's life's plans had taken a detour. She found herself walking along a new and different pathway.

Although her life was busy and full, she found Sam creeping into her thoughts, always with her more and more over the years—his smile, grey eyes, wavy black hair. Five years passed, ten, then fifteen. As she grew older, she began to daydream—to yearn for the boyish charm that she once ridiculed. At odd moments she could hear his voice as if he were in the room, and even awaken at night after all this time and feel the tender warmth of his arms.

Instead of diminishing over time, Sam's image became more well-defined. It bullied her, scoffing at her attempts to ignore and dismiss his existence. His reality had been pushing its way forward to the front line of her thoughts and she was powerless to block it.

She had to see him again—just once—to stop the longing that seemed to overpower her with each passing day. It didn't matter that she was a good wife- a good mother- a good teacher. Time was her enemy. She still missed him. It hurt.

Her recurrent memory was the evenings at dusk at Point Lighthouse. They would lounge on their backs on the lush grass beneath the old jutting structure, staring up at the tower and its vagabond beacon and talk for hours into the night.

"Listen," Sam would whisper in the dark of the night. And she would strain to hear that faint moaning passing over them from the miles of drifting sand below. "Like angels singing," Sam would tell her, "a chorus just for us in the wind and sand."

This thrilling and eerie phenomenon was common knowledge and variously described. The worst of these explanations was the scientific one of echoes and whistles that Sam and Anne would laugh at, the combination of weather, humidity and wind. However, the wind-songs of the sands were legendary and chronicled for many centuries from explorers and poets, to scientists and naturalists.

But Anne secretly never heard the ballad, only pretended to hear, to reassure Sam. She remembered feeling cheated as he'd hum along with it and whispered, "Hear it? Hear it?" And she would say, "Yes, yes."

She would strain to hear even a slight vibration of this famous song that others claimed the wind carried from the dunes, but it was useless. "You must believe," her mother would assure her. "You can't will it to happen. It will come to you when you least expect it. When the gift arrives, it will never leave you. It will be with you always."

Anne sat down on the long grasses and closed her eyes. The winter drafts whipped about and her hair flew wildly about her face. She inhaled the crisp coastal sea air and let her mind wander back in time. To the beginning.

She and Sam were fourteen when they swore they would forever be best friends. Anne remembered this solemn pact solidified with a hug-and-a-half and the two rings they exchanged, made from rolled aluminum foil. While other teenagers in the area traveled in groups, Samuel Banks and Anne Campbell were inseparable. Nothing could have kept them apart.

On lazy summer days, the two spent hours at Sam's beach house listening to records, playing their favorite songs over and over. They would eat pistachio nuts as they sat side-by-side on the front porch, cracking open the shells. Their fingers were forever stained red after eating handfuls of the salted nuts. By the end of the afternoon, empty bottles of cola and piles of discarded shells were scattered about them.

On summer nights they ran barefoot across the wet sand, chasing the evening tide, their bodies often weak from skipping and jumping, breathless from laughter. Then, they would collapse, laying on their backs on cold sand at the water's edge. As the night sea crept over their exhausted forms, it drenched them, causing them to sputter and squeal. Innocent fun, Anne knew, but much more: an invisible bond between them that kept them close. Sacred and privileged.

They never ridiculed each other or their individual dreams. Sam could tell her anything almost by just thinking it. The same was true of her. Their friendship grew with an intensity so strong, neither could fathom a life apart from the other. Was it real love, Anne wondered? She wasn't sure. All she knew was that she cherished each moment they spent together.

At seventeen, their relationship changed as they matured into young adults, both blossoming strong and winsome. Sam's eyes were a deeper grey, the color of the winter sea. He stood well above Anne now, hovering over her head, she thought sometimes as if blocking intrusions from the outside world. Their teasing, their flirtatious bantering evolved into a raw chemistry that connected them, bouncing back and forth between their youthful souls.

Anne found herself blushing when Sam put his arms around her for the first time as mature bodied adults and held her tightly. She tried to picture their lives together as adults.

"When you return from school, we'll build our beach house," he promised. "Then have a dozen kids running free over these miles of white sand."

On her eighteenth birthday Sam gave her a silver heart with their names engraved on the back which she wore on a chain. Their kisses were lingering now, truthful and passionate.

Anne remembered that day she stood on the bluff at the lighthouse waiting for Sam with the letter of acceptance to college in Boston. They sat close together looking out at the vast body of water before them, watching the blankets of white foam roll in to shore around the jagged rocks.

He would not stand in her way, he told her, and hoped the time would pass by quickly, then said, "Congratulations," and kissed her cheek.

"You know I'll be back," she assured him, turning from his red eyes and gazing back over the Pacific.

"Goodbye and hello again," she said out loud, now standing on that same bluff, the Point Lighthouse in the distance. She began towards it, hearing her heart pound, rehearsing what had been rehearsed countless times. "Oh, hi, Sam, do you remember our foil rings? Our hug-and-a-half? Or have I alone grown up silly and sentimental?"

Then, she saw him—the lone figure standing near the lighthouse, tossing stones off the cliff to the water below. A youth of fourteen, with black wavy hair, and she knew even at that distance his eyes were grey like the December Sea. His movements mesmerized her, called her back, to a boy maneuvering into the self—assured posture of a man-to-be, in the very same spot on the grass under the beacon. She stared at this fraternal form, whose manner and movements were like her own, long ago.

She dared not move forward lest she jar that sacred vision of youth. She was frozen as she feasted on the boy's presence and prayed that he would not turn and see her. For if he did and walked away, she would wail at the broken spell. She took a deep breath and cried inaudibly at her breach in time. It looked and felt the same.

Tears flowed. Her eyes unblinking.

From the side she sensed someone approaching, making his way up the trail from the beach house. The adult figure continued nearer, but Anne would not turn to it. Instead, she kept her eyes on the boy, drinking in his timeless picture. Until the boy turned, and cried out, "Dad!" And waved his hand at the approaching adult.

As the figure approached, Anne stepped back in shock.

"Hey!" she heard him call, but she would not look, instead she stepped further back, two steps for his every one.

She would not look at his face, the face of a ghost. Ghosts were invisible, invisible they should stay.

Her eyes still remained on the boy as the boy approached the man.

Then, she turned on her heels and ran back, down the winding dirt trails towards her car.

The voice called her name. She ignored it. Soon its echo lost strength as she made her way away from the bluff. Anne reached her car and sat inside, trying to catch her breath. The voice was gone. It was quiet. The waves were calm, frothing peacefully under the setting sun.

Her eyes were dry, her head clear. And then...she heard it, the sound coming from the sea of drifting sand. It was a whistle, a moan- a chorus of faint violins. It played to the dusk, and to the flat grey Oregon sky that was streaked with blue and yellow remnants from the sun's farewell glare.

Anne sat silent, drinking in the wind's serenade.

"Merry Christmas to me," she breathed, grateful for the season's first gift.

It was the gift of the song and the gift of her past and she had captured it all. Now, so fresh in her mind she could put the past to rest, where it belonged: in a special place in her heart.

Anne turned the car around and headed back. The wind serenade followed, carrying with it the mystical refrain from the dunes. For centuries it had played for others and now it had found Anne. It would stay with her now... forever, in song and in spirit.

Rightful Journey

He was lost in the fog, its thickness misting his senses, its clouds enveloping his eyes, blinding him. Jeremiah was sailing in circles, deliberately, as if allowing its force to determine his destination. He stood up, steadying himself on the platform of his catamaran, and lifted his face to the salty spray as it blew past.

Though a skilled, often bold, navigator, today his hands fumbled and his mind was as clouded as the blanket of moist air that surrounded him. Not that he cared. It had been his decision to keep the craft out on these low-visibility waters, knowing full well of the ominous fog bank creeping in his direction. But he was running—hurting and angry at God and the family he left behind.

"Damn you all!!" He shouted to nothingness ahead of him, his sputters dying in the fog, dissipated and unacknowledged by the gulls that glided and swooped down from above.

"Congratulations! You will be a Daddy soon!" He played the happy voices over again in his mind—the shouts of joy from friends and well-wishers back at his village a lifetime ago.

His wife Mara was about to give birth to their first child. When word spread that the couple were about to be parents, flowers and gifts were brought to their small simple brick-and-bamboo home.

Jeremiah and Mara were married in Florida. Soon after, they moved to East Africa, to the thriving harbor between Kenya and Mozambique they called home. It bordered the Indian Ocean and was an outlet for the mainland's agricultural and mineral exports. Consequently, jobs were plentiful. They thrived. They purchased a sailboat and Jeremiah made his living visiting ports along the coast, selling coffee, cotton and tobacco. They soon adapted to the hot and humid climate, almost as quickly as Mara learned to read and write Swahili and Arabic, which enabled her to find work as an English teacher to the children in the village.

The noisy colorful international harbor where Jeremiah worked loading his boat with consumer goods was visited by people from all nations, some from the other side of the planet, all of whom traveled by rail or by sea to barter for their wares. Nicknamed "The Port Of Many Faces," the harbor was a plethora of skin colors and languages. So much was the diversity that the language of the harbor became universal: a language of simple gestures—a nod, a pat on the back, a smile.

On the day in which Mara went into labor, Jeremiah heard the busy chatter of the port in the distance as he sat on the steps outside his home. He winced for her pain, at the length of her prolonged labor which was lasting longer than expected. He overheard the doctor on the phone calling for an assistant to come help with the delivery of the child.

If it was a little girl, he knew Mara's spirits would soar. But deep in his heart Jeremiah prayed for a boy. He yearned for a son who would travel the magic seas with him. What greater pleasure could a man attain than to share the vast ocean with his own flesh and blood, he asked himself, a lean and strong boy— directing the sails to the wind....inhaling the salty sea spray....laughing with his old man under an invigorating summer sun. Together he and his son would visit the ports along the coast, bartering with friends old and new. And at night, drifting under a black sky, they would make wishes over stars shooting across the heavens. And during these private moments they would share their innermost thoughts, hopes, dreams.

"There were some complications," the doctor explained as he stood before Jeremiah. "She had a rough time, but the baby was delivered safely. I'm sorry," he hesitated, "but Mara may not be able to carry another child in the future."

The words stung. The doctor asked Jeremiah if he would like to see his wife and his son. It took time for the new father to comprehend the words through the cloud of sadness and disbelief. But then the words did register. "His son!" He walked inside and stood looking at his wife who cradled the tiny infant in a blanket. He embraced both. Mara held the bundle up and presented their child to his father.

Jeremiah's arms trembled when he took his son, but smiled at the black tufts of hair on the tiny golden-brown face.

"He has your eyes," Mara said.

Jeremiah seemed not to hear her. "You will learn to sail before you learn to walk, my son," Jeremiah spoke softly. "Welcome to the world. Your name will be James Joseph after each of your grandfathers. But we will call you Jimmy Jo."

Jeremiah held the boy to his breast to enable him to hear the steady beat of his heart, and to punctuate the bond to his son he already felt. He vowed to protect this fragile gift, but it would not be for long. For with every year of growth would come a milestone. The child, he knew, would blossom in strength until he was prepared to embark on his rightful journey.

Sadly, as the months passed, these milestones were slow in coming. The boy lagged far behind his peers—his muscles soft, his coordination undeveloped, his movements slow and awkward. And he was quiet, spiritless: Where was the wailing? The fits of laughter? The demands for food? Jeremiah wondered as he watched his Jimmy Jo play quietly, too placid, too content. At one year he was not able to sit up on his own. At two he had yet to take his first step.

Fear haunted Jeremiah and Mara as they watched their boy's slow, stunted progress. Wait and see they were told. Have patience.

After many trips to the doctor, a specialist was able to finally make a diagnosis. "James has a rare genetic disease. It will affect his normal development. He will never walk and there will be other problems to overcome as well. I am truly sorry."

In the days and months that followed, Jeremiah watched his wife become the strong one. She held her tears in check with a fierce maternal instinct that knew no bounds. With spirit and love she was forever at her little Jimmy Jo's side, feeding him, bathing him and speaking to him in song and prayer.

In private, Jeremiah mourned the loss of the child who would never share his life's dream. His visions of father and son sailing the seas with great strength and bravery would never be realized. As hard as he tried, Jeremiah could not seem to come to terms with the future that lay before him as he watched his son struggle through even the most minimal tasks.

His days at the harbor grew longer, as did his trips along the coast. Shamed by the final realization that he did not want to return home because of his son, his moods became black and sullen. Through darkness and storms he sailed haphazardly, shoving the rudder one way, then another, altering the craft's direction willy-nilly as it zig-zagged sharply across the waters.

"I am Jeremiah, the sailor! A father without a heart!!" He yelled to God and the wind. "What man walks away from a helpless child because it hurts to cast eyes upon him?" He cried to himself, then turned to the sky. "Create and deliver your most furious storm if you wish! Show me your wrath, your lightning, your giant waves!"

The waves did not appear, but the fog bank crept in and eerily wrapped its murky haze around Jeremiah. It settled so near that it erased even the colorful sail that whipped about above him in the wind.

Immersed in the blanket of moist air Jeremiah took his knife and pried the compass from its wooden panel and tossed it out to sea. There! he thought, now there's no way of telling where I'm headed. East? South? What difference does it make? This thought comforted him since he was lost anyway, in will. And spirit.

Day turned into night, night into day, and still the fog stayed. It had trapped Jeremiah in a tight cocoon — suspending him in time and space. He felt no fear. He felt it was where he belonged — in a vacuum, in nothingness. In time hunger and thirst nagged at him, his body weak and slumped against the hull while the winds took control of the sails.

"I will drift until I drown, as long as it takes," he told himself, knowing he could never return, could no longer pretend he was mighty. For he was no longer a man, he finally admitted. A man walks alongside his wife to face life's challenges and adversities. A man holds his child in his arms with joyful love, not with sadness and pity.

Jeremiah saw the question in Mara's eyes. Why? How could he answer her when he had to stifle the words that he wanted to scream: "Let's turn back the clock—start over and make it right." There was no one to blame. He had tried. He blamed himself. He blamed Mara and the doctor. Even the child. But he knew his sweet and gentle child was innocent, an angel loved by all in the village.

He heard the words of the children in the fog, as if mocking his mood. "We are here to play with Jimmy Jo," the children sang, "We have presents for him..." And he recalled their daily gifts to his son—a used toy, a book, a candy treat—to which his child would respond, not in the words he lacked, but in his precious smile—his gratefulness relayed by the inner light that shone through knowing eyes. Those saintly eyes sparkled the peace and joy his son felt within. And when his son would look at his father, he would turn and look away. Somehow, the boy's eyes reached into his soul and recognized his fear. And understood. And forgave. The sea calmed, its waves rocking Jeremiah in soothing motion, like a cradle. He started once again to doze, only to awaken to a hard knocking sound on the side of the boat. Peering through the fog just a few feet away, he saw two bottleneck dolphins gracefully break the surface, blowing and grunting. A mother and her calf, he saw, probably herding schools of fish to obtain food. Jeremiah knew these seas were plentiful with mackerel, yellowtail and squid. He watched as, keeping close to the boat, they submerged and reappeared over and over, mesmerizing him as they danced about in the water. A fitting performance.

Jeremiah leaned over the side to get a closer look. The mother was a flawless beauty, her bluish-grey body sleek and streamlined. She had clear and happy eyes. She disappeared, then popped up out of the water awaiting the sailor's acknowledgment. He reached out his hand and she let him pat her. He expected her to flee, but she stayed.

"Lucky one," he told her. "You were born to roam the open seas."

He closed his eyes and once again dipped his hand down to pat her leathery skin. Quickly he yanked his hand back. He looked in the water and saw it was her calf he had touched, and when he had, his hand brushed over a thick jagged piece of flesh. When he saw it was the remnants of an open wound, he jumped back. And when he saw the calf in full-view, he recoiled. Never before had he seen such a pathetic creature — torn apart from nose to tail. The result of a shark attack, no less. How could it have survived? he asked himself in horror. The poor creature's body was shredded in raw, gaping wounds, some of which had healed to rubbery scars. Open sockets on each side of his head were empty, his eyes gone. And through all Jeremiah's shock and horror, the calf blew spray and danced in a circle, his antics watched and appreciated by his watchful his mother.

Still Jeremiah stared. Could it still suckle? Jeremiah wondered, noticing that part of his nose was ripped to the side, broken and shredded in ugly strips of flesh.

Jeremiah turned his back on the monster, hoping it would disappear into the fog that surrounded them. But the mother would not hear of it...she would not allow the sailor to recoil in disgust. She squealed and jumped and pounded the water sending hard, drenching waves over Jeremiah's body.

"He lives!" she seemed to shout. "See my beautiful child. He too, is of God's creation!"

Jeremiah wondered at his abrupt relief at the fog. Was the fog's thick blanket protecting him from the prying eyes of the sea birds who would have been amused at his cowardice of horror. The sailor found himself curling into a fetal ball, the seas rising suddenly and throwing themselves up on the deck. Meanwhile, he thought he could hear the gulls laughing at him. He clutched at his sides, sputtering and cursing. "I'm dreaming!" he screamed. "What mortal can hear a sea creature speak and a bird laugh?"

Then, all was still. He rose and looked over at the splashes of their tail fins, side by side, as they disappeared from view.

Jeremiah wondered how long the calf, blind and broken, would survive in the dangerous waters. Forever, he figured. For not a shark or killer whale stood a chance with his mother protector at his side. Her eyes were his guide, her heart, his shield.

Like Mara, Jeremiah thought. Not much difference. Mara shadowed James from hardship and danger, yet let him dance in his own light without interference. She relished in his sweetness and charm and proudly presents him to all as the pure and deserving soul that he is. They are strong ones, Jeremiah acknowledged. A hurting dolphin...a bird not yet ready to leave the nest...are not abandoned. How easy it is to run. How little effort it takes to hide and be true to only the strong and steady. It is the weak, like me, who turn away. It is the weak who find solace in the false idea of perfection when they lack even a fraction of the spirit of the humble.

A flush of heat and anger crept though Jeremiah's body. His eyes hardened with a new determination. How selfish to think that I could hoard the magic of the ocean for only the fit and able to enjoy. He recalled the look of delight on his son's face when a sudden summer rain fell, splashing warm drops upon his nose, and when his black eyes widened at the sight of the sun as it set in a glowing ball of fire.

My child will know the thrill of sailing the waters, Jeremiah promised. We will sail and I will be honored to have him by my side. If he cannot stand, he will sit. If he cannot sit, I will hold him safe within my arms. And still, he will know the feeling of sea air as it filters through every pore of his body. If he cannot yell, only whisper, I will speak for him. I will join him in laughter and we will wish together on stars that shoot across the night sky. My wishes will be for his happiness. And for many days ahead with my boy, watching our sails arch high in the wind.

Jeremiah's thoughts became sharp and clear and a new strength caused him to rise. He stood tall and steady. Through the mist he saw Mara's face, her eyes beckoning... sweet and forgiving. A ray of sun broke through from above. The yellow glare opened a narrow pathway, a guide out if he needed it.

But he didn't. Jeremiah knew the way. With a sharp turn of the rudder, he altered the boat's direction. It gained speed under the force of the wind and its commander. Jeremiah the sailor, used his heart as a navigator and it led him home. To the Port of Many Faces and a boy named Jimmy Jo.

Keeper of the Home

John Williams stood at the crossroads of Moss Point, a lively fishing and crabbing town in Virginia's Northern Neck Peninsula. "Left or right?" he wondered, looking up at the darkening sky. The summer night was warm and humid in this quaint scenic coastal town, but in the morning, he would be on a plane home to a very different town — Dallas — and to the high-pressured job that brought him out here. To perform like a puppet, he thought, as he had just hours before to the buyers at the tire plant. He was exhausted.

After the meeting John had returned to his motel room off Main Street, next to the Maritime Museum and Antique Shop. He changed into jeans and an old pair of sneakers, then walked a block to the corner tavern and drank four beers with the locals. The liquor buzzed his senses, and not used to so many, John felt unsteady on his feet as he stumbled outside the tavern into the sultry night. He went for a walk, making his way through the neighborhoods of the unfamiliar town.

Left, he decided, then right, John strode, up one winding street and down another, stumbling in unsteady steps as he stopped to examine a bush or a fence in need of repair. In the distance the sky seemed somehow ominous, and would smolder with occasional white flashes of heat- lightening.

It was inhumanly quiet. Unconsciously, John dug into his pockets for his portable phone, feeling only emptiness. It was gone. For a moment he panicked, realizing his pager, even his wallet, too, were back in his room at the motel. What if Elaine tried to reach him? What if his boss called with a urgent last minute message? He paused and thought it over, then realized he was suddenly free of these electronic leashes that led him around. For the first time in many years, he was alone and unreachable. He was scared. And excited. And alive.

A dog barked in the distance as the fifty-year-old man whooped and chuckled, dancing in circles on cracked stretches of sidewalk in the middle of nowhere. For over an hour he walked, past a schoolhouse painted with chalk graffiti and a vacant gas station that had seen better days. "I'm lost but I don't care," he sang to the streetlight and then kicked a rusty bicycle that had been tossed alongside a dirt path. He felt carefree and young again as he skipped along clumsily. But the alcohol played havoc with his equilibrium and he stumbled awkwardly to the ground.

With a smile John picked himself up, then walked in circles, following one path, then another. Ahead lay narrow dirt pathways and gravel roads lined with trees whose branches swooped down and danced about in the summer night breeze. Deeper into the semi-darkness he strode into the east wind until he found himself in an opening at the ocean's edge.

John stood looking across the vast sea, moon-tinted green. He watched the waves' foamy whitecaps shine under slivers of moonlight, then disappear, only to surface again and again. Off to the right he noticed a field of wild flowers and heard a chorus of frogs singing. John walked across the field towards an orange-yellow light that glowed in the distance. As he came closer to the source of the light, he saw it shone from a large white clapboard cottage with a front porch and swing.

A woman sat on the swing. She waved to him, beckoning.

"This is crazy," he screamed, realizing his voice was a mere whisper against the crash of the waves as they slammed upon shore. "I'm trespassing on someone's property in the middle of the night. I could end up in jail." But while John's conscious mind scolded him, his tired legs brought him closer to the porch on their own accord, and closer to the beautiful woman on the swing.

Suddenly he stood before her and stared. He couldn't help it. She smiled. "I'm Belle," she said in a voice sweet and shy. She was like an angel, dressed only in a soft white robe which fluttered in the breeze, as she moved in slow-motion to the side of the swing to make room for John to sit and rest. A strong scent of jasmine permeated the air as the frog's chorus serenaded them in their silence. If this was a dream, he wanted to wake up. He wondered what Elaine, his wife, would say if she saw him sitting here next to this magnificent woman in the late-night hours.

He looked down to his red and swollen wrist and realized he was pinching himself as if to test his wakefulness. He saw his wrist was starting to bruise. He knew he was more awake than he had ever been in his life.

He looked over at the woman just a foot away on the swing. "My name is John Williams and I'm in town on business. I took an evening walk and must've lost my way," he said, and immediately sensed her amusement.

He looked down, embarrassed, but her silence somehow made him want to talk more. So, in the next few minutes, he chattered on and on about himself and his life. As he talked, she nodded and smiled in implicit acceptance. And this was all he needed for his words to flow as if dammed up for so long.

He told her about his family, about his two teenage boys. He told her they had somehow lost their way, experimenting with drugs and living wild and aimless lives. And he was powerless to stop them. He told her about his wife Elaine, describing her stress and her preoccupation with her job as a stockbroker. Techno-wife he called her. She was married to her computer, he said, where she spent hours talking to strangers across the world — never much to him anymore.

"What about you?" he thought he heard her whisper, not sure if the heard her correctly, or at all.

John chattered on, unloading his unhappiness and despair. He told her of his health problems, his anxiety, his allergies, high blood pressure, ulcers and battles with excess weight. He mentioned his daily pills, naming each one by name as if friends, as he counted them on his fingers. When he ran out of fingers, he put his hands down, realizing that he had been talking non-stop. Embarrassed, John jumped off the swing and paced back and forth across the wooden porch.

From a more comfortable distance, he looked at Belle appraisingly. He could not help but compare her with his wife. What had happened to Elaine over the years, he wondered, so stick-thin from dieting and hidden under layers of heavy make-up. Her once rich chestnut-brown hair was now a bleached unnatural yellow and her once natural hands were now hideously adorned with long witch-like false nails, each studded with cheap diamond chips. She was once like Belle, he thought, so fresh and natural. When they first met, Elaine had a raw beauty and an innocence that made him want to embrace and protect her forever. But somehow, somewhere along the way she hardened. She became cold and distant as they both spiraled into, and were overcome by, a competitive materialistic world. They existed in the same space, yet were so busy as to be virtual strangers to each other.

And him? In John's relentless need "to make a living," he told Belle, he, too, had lost his way. Nowadays he had no highs or lows—no dreams. It seemed each family member was involved with his own wants and needs, his own survival to the exclusion of every other member. And so John lived his life with out-of-control kids and a self-absorbed wife. John looked over at Belle suddenly, thinking, then saying, that he had never really thought about all this. Until tonight. Tonight, his thoughts were out, exposed. He had put them in words.

Belle held out her hand and motioned him inside. As they entered, the previous subtle odors of burnt sugar and cinnamon became more pronounced until they entered the kitchen where the home-spun smells enveloped the kitchen air. John closed his eyes with the exquisite smell. He thought he heard children laughing from somewhere in the rooms. Where was her family? he wondered. Her husband? But he did not want to pry as she did not seem to feel talkative.

Shuttered windows reflected the shifting coastal night lights and cast shadows on the salt-bleached floors and walls as they sat at table. John imagined Belle at work in her kitchen, baking delicious cakes and breads for her loved ones. Her demeanor bespoke a soft and loving nature, and John envied the lucky man who was her husband. She was intoxicating. John felt warm and safe and comfortable. He drifted. Soon, his tired eyes felt heavy and began to close.

He jerked awake to sounds of pounding. He quickly scanned his surroundings and realized he was back in his motel room at Moss Point. The annoyed voice of a cab driver reminded him that it was time to leave for the airport. In a whirlwind, John quickly packed, and before he had time to think, he was on a plane headed for home.

Bone-weary and fighting a hangover, John settled back in his seat and closed his eyes. The hum of the plane's engine soon soothed him enough to relax. How did he make it back to the motel? he wondered. In his mind he relived his visit to the clapboard cottage and his meeting with Belle. His body was hurting. But his heart ached. He knew at that moment what he wanted — to become one with nature — to feel pure love again and relive the joyous wonder that his heart had opened to back at that magic dwelling near the sea. He heard the waves pounding in his ears and felt the salt air freshen and tingle every pore of his skin. These feelings would hold him, he thought. But not for long.

John Williams knew he was a changed man, overnight. His senses rejoiced with the ocean sounds, the smells of jasmine, and the chorus of frogs singing across acres of wild flowers leading to the sea. He smiled, recalling the loveliness of Belle.

Never had he ever been so clear-headed and so determined to change the course of his life. He thought of his family: there was time to save them all, if they would just listen. It would be a struggle. How do you pull three headstrong people from their environment and place them in a strange land?

Back home in Dallas, he talked. They listened, but with stone faces. He pleaded. As he did, phones rang, traffic screamed out the window and sounds of sirens competed with his words. He spoke to deaf ears. They shook their heads and pouted and threatened to stay behind. But when they saw he was serious, driven, they became uneasy.

"I want us to be a family again," he told them. "I want to see your beautiful faces smile and hear your laughter. Look at us. We are strangers." John sensed their uneasiness and reluctance, but he promised them over and over that he would bring them to a happier existence.

In late September, he flew to Moss Point ahead of them, looking for property to purchase. For two days he searched the area. As he did, he looked for Belle's clapboard cottage. He wanted to tell her the good news, that his family had finally relented, that all of them were moving to her town. But where was her cottage? He recalled the beers he drank and his fatigue. He wished he had been more clearheaded that night, as he searched, in vain it seemed, for that field of wild flowers and Belle.

A real estate agent drove him through neighborhoods looking for property, but every beach house looked the same. He kept describing the cottage to the agent—the front porch with the swing and shuttered windows—but the loudly dressed agent just stifled a snicker.

Finally, he said, "There is such a home, but it's a long way from here. It's for sale, but it's been vacant for over one hundred years."

John asked the agent to bring him there. He had to see for himself. They parked the car at the edge of a field and walked to an opening that led to the ocean's edge. Off to the right, John saw a broken-down structure in the distance. It looked oddly familiar, but it was barren and lifeless. Even the wild flowers leading up to it were dried and wilted, he saw.

John walked across the field to the front porch of the old house. It was caved in from decay. He kicked a piece of rotting wood and it broke in two, bringing down three more boards with it. The house looked as if it might blow over in a strong wind and John wondered how it withstood the fury of the winter storms. He shook his head in disappointment and started walking back to the agent's car. Suddenly he was stopped frozen with the scent of jasmine floating past. He turned to take a last look at the dilapidated property. The scent of jasmine was replaced by the smell of burnt sugar. This made him doubt his sanity as the house clouded then clarified in his eyes and became so familiar. His eyes lit on a rusty porch-swing discarded and abandoned in a pile of trash.

Reason tugged at his confusion. Perhaps he had walked further that night. Could he have been in another nearby town near the water's edge? John looked around and thought of the hard work that would be needed to bring this property back to life. Then, he smiled. For he knew just the family that could make it happen. "I'll take it!" he yelled to the agent, whose mouth dropped open in surprise.

In the months that followed the Williams family worked to make their house a home. It wasn't easy. They labored from first light to the night hours. The boys swept, pounded and painted under John's direction. Their skin turned brown in the autumn sun and their eyes were clear and focused. The porch was soon reconstructed and a new swing was built.

Elaine was quiet at first, but soon found that she loved her kitchen. She began cooking and baking and was excited by the way she was rediscovering and re-mastering her culinary skills. The smells of burnt sugar and cinnamon enveloped the kitchen air. With her discovery of the art of gardening, she began to neglect her precious computer. In time, it found a home in the basement while Elaine watched her rows of vegetables and herbs grow.

Each afternoon when the tide came close to the rocks, she stood facing the ocean, her hands planted at her hips. With her face turned up to the sun, she drank in the warmth of the rays and salty sea air, feeling healthy and strong.

Elaine's pale face was now pink, glowing and freckled, her hair returned to rich chestnut, and her makeup and false nails a dinosaur of another eon. As for John, his ailments faded, and with them, the variety of pills he used to take to keep his body in motion. He felt himself growing stronger with each passing day.

But each day he regretted that he could not share his happiness with Belle, could not show her how much he had changed. He wanted her to see how his family was blossoming and to thank her for saving their lives.

But he did not know he did not have to go far to thank Belle. She was with him every minute of every day, watching over him and his beautiful family. At night, when they lay cozy in their beds, lulled to sleep by the sound of the waves pounding the shore, Belle's spirit hovered above them. She floated about through the house, sometimes stopping to sit on the swing and rock back and forth on the front porch.

Her nurturing soul was so strong that when it was her time to pass over a century ago, she could not bear to exit the living world completely until she found just the right person to take her place. "Keeper of the Home" people used to call her. But she didn't mind. She so loved taking care of her family, cooking for them, wiping away their tears and loving them unconditionally. The magic of living at the sea's edge had kept them healthy, in mind and spirit. She could never turn her domain over to just anyone. She wanted someone who shared her very thoughts. Someone who stood confident, absorbing daily the secrets of nature's beauty and storing that knowledge in her heart, to borrow from and learn.

Belle had found her replacement in Elaine. The clapboard cottage had transformed this woman into a giving being, filled with new love and compassion for her family and the sea. Belle knew that she and her husband and two boys would thrive and live happily here for many years.

Belle made one last check on each of them, sleeping soundly in their beds. She bade Elaine a silent farewell and turned her home over to her. The wild flowers glowed once again under the glare of the autumn moon and the frogs sang their chorus in unison.

Belle smiled. She could not have hoped for more. In a split second she was gone, back to her own family, who had been waiting so patiently for her return.

Faith and Forgiveness

Pulsating neon lights in greens, blues, and purples blinded Dave at the front entrance to the carnival. In the midst of the dazzling, flickering colors, circus music piped through scratchy speakers. These calliope clamors competed with the overture of screams and shouts and frenzied laughter emanating from the thrill rides adjacent the midway. The night was thick and hot and palpable.

Dave snuck a glance at his wife, Faith. She looked dazzling dressed in her favorite tight blue jeans which cuffed the tops of her brown suede boots. Her hair was tucked under a sleek new blue cowboy hat. Silver earrings dangling from her ears translated the brash colors of the midway to quiet loveliness. When she noticed his look, she looped her arm through his, pulling him close to her and smiled light-heartedly.

Dave looked away involuntarily. His heart was strained, his mood turning even more tense and sullen. Her innocent charm exacerbated the torture he was feeling, only moments into the festivity. He knew her exhilaration was doomed. This would be their last night together. He had to tell her. Tonight. He had to leave Nashville to embark on a long overdue lone-journey back home. It was time to say goodbye.

A fisherman by trade, 'home' to Captain Dave Miller was the central coast of California. Indeed, for half of his thirty-five years he had fished for Salmon and Rock Cod along the coastal waters of the Pacific. Images of his past life assailed him through the canned band music. The screaming circus crowd only served to isolate his thoughts. He had memories of looking into the eye of a Mighty Blue Whale, of hand feeding sea lions, of swimming with dolphins. From an early age, he knew he had been married to the sea. He pronounced his vows of matrimony on more than one occasion, sometimes standing on his boat on a sun-drenched afternoon, at others drifting afloat in darkness after an autumn storm. This marriage was a life commitment, freely entered, an equal pact, albeit a surrender to Mother Ocean's mysticism and virtue.

The ocean enchanted. She was gorgeous in a broad sense, but it was not her physical beauty that enthralled him. Rather it was the dimensions of her personality that chained him, kept his interest piqued. She could be loving and calm one moment-angry, dismal the next. Some days she would coddle him, keeping him anchored by her soothing rhythm, only to ignore him on other days while flirting with others, dismissing Dave with callous disregard. He withstood the pain. But there were times he tried to leave her.

On one of these occasions, he managed to stay away from her for several months. But he returned. Always, he returned. He was like a curious pup who would scamper away uncertainly, testing perhaps, but ever finding his way back home. On returning he would not have to explain. There was no need. Likewise, no need to interpret his joy upon returning, as if one could explain the free feeling of the wind upon his face, or the salt taste in the undulating waves. These sense impressions were self-explanatory, lessons in themselves. She was worth coming home to. He could wander, yes, but he could never fully abandon her, for even she had an invisible line drawn in the sand.

He knew there was an unspoken alliance built on such force, one to be reckoned with. And so, he stayed close, meanwhile existing in his land-locked middle world where he worked hard and played harder. His marriage with the sea was a good marriage, one he believed destined to persevere, timeless.

Then, he met Faith.

It seemed so innocent an encounter, that time, years ago, when Dave flew to Nashville to visit his sister Lee. He stayed a few days. On his way back to the airport he stopped for a drink. The dim-lit bar was crammed with noisy people, the air dense with stale smoke. He sat next to a young woman at the bar — slim and cute, he thought. Her infectious smile became captivating. She wore it well and sincerely on her heart-shaped face and pretty blue eyes.

"My name's Faith." She extended her hand.

He took it, and without realizing it, held on to it, locking it in his own for more than the acceptable first-acquaintance shake. Her hand didn't tense up or withdraw, her eyes didn't waver. She was a secretary, she said. In minutes he learned she was single and lived alone in an apartment downtown.

During a lull in the conversation, Dave remembered, how the rain started, at first a light drizzle, only to become sheets hammering against the windows. He recalled how distracted he was by the tempest, how his eyes riveted to the window, until he felt Faith's soft fingers turn his face from the glass and she smiled. Faith put a handful of quarters in the jukebox and they lulled off again, this time Dave's eyes on Faith's face, listening to Nashville crooners plying their magical trade.

The two new friends sat in quiet, drinking beer, contented in their shared space. He wanted to know more of her story, her life and her work. But talk didn't seem right at this crossroad. Instead, he asked her to dance.

They clung to each other, two strangers, careening on the small section of dance floor to an array of country ballads from Willie, Garth, Johnny, oblivious to all around them. It wasn't until two in the morning that Dave realized he had missed his flight back home. He didn't know where he was, what words were spoken, or what happened that night. He did know he fell in love with a wondrous woman. It wasn't the liquor, it wasn't the conversation or music or the sweet rainy coziness of the dim bar, or her beauty. It was her. She had led him home with her. Dave stayed. For five years.

"Buy me a Cotton Candy, Captain," she purred into his ear, tugging at his arm as she led him through a obstacle course of cowboys and clowns.

Pitchmen yelled at them as they passed, daring him to throw a dart and win a prize for his lady. She directed him to a booth where they stood and shared a colossal cloud of pink sugar spun from a machine. As it dissolved in his mouth, Dave thought it sweeter than anything he had ever tasted. The spun sugar permeated the air around them. With sticky fingers Faith pulled his face close to hers and kissed him.

His words, long rehearsed and overdue, lingered on his lips, but he pulled them back before they tumbled. He couldn't, not now, not while she was gazing at him, feeding him this sweet-smelling cloud of confection her fingers were toying off the paper stick.

Hands entwined Dave and Faith zigzagged through the midway gauntlet, over gravelly pathways of asphalt covered with sawdust, giggling at comical signs announcing, "Come and see the Alligator Woman! Half human, half reptile." They gawked at the pictures displayed on side show banners depicting the oddities to be found inside.

"Championship Rodeo inside," an old man called to them. "Biggest names from Oklahoma and Texas. Come in and see the Daredevil Rider...the Trick Roper."

Faith found the Bandstand where she pulled Dave down next to her on the front row bench. Willie Nelson and his band was featured that night free of charge. As they played, she sang his ballads out loud, caught up in the music and the moment. He wondered if this might be a good time to tell her, while her favorite country singer serenaded her. Her obvious mellow and spirit mood might buffet her from what he was about to tell her–might allay her broken heart.

He turned to her but she took his arm and jumped up. "Let's take a ride on the Roller Coaster!"

She led him to the Midway. He held her as the coaster sped over ancient looking tracks, dipping and turning. After it dropped them one hundred feet, he could not even conjure the words he wanted to speak. His head was spinning. He limped off the ride and clung to Faith, waiting over twenty minutes until the dizziness subsided.

Guilt tormented him. He knew she was his strength when he needed it. She did not complain or burden him with any insecurities. From the first morning he woke in her bed, dazed and confused, she never insisted that he stay. The door was always open, she told him. But when he walked through the following days, he stumbled into an atmosphere of domesticity that felt new and gratifying. She introduced him to a unfamiliar life, a city life, and he was soon mixing in the buzz of song and society.

Into his second year he asked her to marry him. She accepted. They declared their vows in a small chapel in rural Tennessee. Over the years he would think of leaving, feeling he had been gone too long. At times he yearned for his home back at the wharf, where his sea bird friends circled the overhead skies as colorful tourists dallied along the boardwalk tasting fresh roasted garlic, clam chowder and smoked salmon. He missed the freedom of drifting alone under the stars, once again. The sea had been calling all these years, while he feigned deafness. But he knew he heard her, that he was slowly giving in to her summons.

I'm a coward, he thought, strapped into a car in the total darkness of the Haunted House. Faith dug her nails into his arm and hung on as they bolted through hairpin turns and zig-zag curves. She screamed when a green ghost flew over their heads. In the midst of the deafening screeches and howls he managed the half-hearted courage to finally utter, "Faith, I am going back home. Tonight. I'm leaving you, returning to my boat and my life at sea."

Of course, she did not hear him. His words were lost in the pandemonium, in her squeals and the screams of children. But he spoke them as if practicing for the upcoming moment they would be heard, standing brutally on their own.

They stopped to share an ear of corn, grilled and buttery, seasoned with hot sauce and lime. Her face was flushed and beaming, her body tremors thrilling to Dave as if she were once again a teenager on her first date.

He turned her face to his. "You look beautiful," he said.

"I love you," she replied.

The words seemed to fall so easily off her tongue and caught him off-guard. She looked radiant amidst the backdrop of colored lights. It was how he wanted to remember her, he thought, exactly how she looked at this very moment, when he was miles away, drifting the open seas.

It was time, Dave decided. He grabbed her and took her in his arms. As he started to speak, she took off her hat and nuzzled her face in the space under his chin and melted into him.

His jaw locked over his words. It was useless. He would have to slip away now, knowing he can never tell her the words he feels he has to. She would search for him and worry and cry. But he would write her a letter, and detail his heart when he was in the safety of distance, safe from her gentleness and pretty blue eyes.

Dave pushed her away gently and turned to leave. She grabbed his hand and held on. When he tried to pull away, she tightened her grasp and at that moment he realized that she knew. It wasn't going to be easy. Her heart-shaped face was pale. She stared at him. The knife had entered on its own, piercing under its own power. For what, he wondered? Was it worth this? Was the sea and the past and his one- time home worth hurting someone whose only fault was loving him? Perhaps not. Perhaps it was only a myth he had been tormenting over...just a spot on the map he had longed for, then fashioned to emerge mortal over time.

He was torn, between two women, the one who stood before him, and the one he left behind. He wondered if the latter would wait—forgive him if he stayed a while longer.

Dave figured Mother Sea had her pick of men to beguile with her seductive rhythms, men younger than him, stronger, more courageous— hundreds, thousands more. Men who were free, unlike him.

Maybe one day he would bring Faith to meet her and she would be welcomed not with jealousy but with compassion and recognition. He would take her on the waters. Then, she might understand his former life.

Until then, there was still much to look forward to. The night was young. Willie was singing, his nomadic twang belting out, "Good-Hearted Woman," over the cheers of the crowd.

Amidst ringing bells and neon signs, Dave gathered his wife in his arms. They danced, that night, under a dark blanket of Tennessee sky. All around them children laughed. Lights exploded. And the air tasted sweet, like Cotton Candy.

Embracing Grace

"I hope to uncover the magic that lies in these ordinary waters- that soothes the soul and brings forth spontaneous song and laughter. I would like to know how the waters can sustain hope in the hearts of those whose misfortune it is to live with sufferings of human kind."

Grace Harrison

July 20, 1832

The evening was sultry. Its thick air hung heavy over the land, wilting the leaves of the ancient oak trees into moist curls. These oaks surrounded the Harrison Plantation, a noble estate that sprawled over six hundred acres of land. At its north end were the modest wooden cabins that housed a dozen slaves. The oppressive heat didn't discriminate — it smothered rich and poor alike, even the three-storied Greek-porticoed Harrison house.

The entire property lay along the black waters of a swamp stream that meandered through Chester County, South Carolina, as it made its way to the Atlantic Ocean. The thick forest was dominated by hickory and pine, these trees most prevalent in the areas bordering the swamp, so dense in places along the murky waters that the land never saw sunlight.

Grace Harrison, the mistress of the plantation, rested in the sitting room near the front window of her mansion. From time to time she blotted her flushed face with a linen handkerchief. Her movements, as always, were quick and nervous, but ever prim and proper. Grace at thirty stood almost six-foot, a tall woman for her day, she knew. Her slimness tempered her height, but her brown hair was ever and severely secured at the top of her head with ivory hair pins. Her pointed nose and thin lips, often pursed, seemed to set off a frown permanently etched across her face, as if anticipating some new aggravation.

Her favorite aggravation, especially now in this heat, were the nightly songs and chants she heard coming from the waters downstream. She bristled at the voices, piqued that her laborers could find humor, let alone such vocal strength at the end of a grueling day. Yet she heard them, knowing how they cajoled nightly around each other, splashed in the cloudy waters near their cabins, and sang hymns that resounded high above the trees.

Grace spent many an hour mulling over her minor torments. Friendless and without suitors, she claimed to like it that way, living her life according to her own lights, a practical business woman, a proper lady. She ate her meals alone prepared by her two domestic servants that she brought over from the cabins-Rose, sixteen and the younger sister Selena who just entered her thirteenth year.

Such was Grace's lonely routine since the death of her father of pneumonia last year and her sudden inheritance of the Harrison estate.

She recalled his whispered words, as if yesterday. "Take care of the place, my dear," he said, his once robust frame now so small in the four-poster bed. " I am going to join your mother where we will wait for you."

She promised to carry on as he took his final breaths, murmuring, "Yes, Father," and kissed his forehead at the same moment his body shuddered and then became still.

As she clutched, then loosened her grip, on his hand, she recalled the cry that escaped her lips, her grief and her despair that she was truly alone. She stiffened with the sudden responsibility: a thriving plantation where they raised corn, wheat and tobacco. This overwhelming responsibility included not only her stewardship of the land, but her management of the Thatchers, a family of slaves who worked the fields and cultivated the crops—hoeing, plowing and planting—from dawn to dusk.

The Thatcher family's Patriarch was Josiah, whom her father had delegated to the back quarters of the main house long ago. His primary task was calling the others to and from labor, and assigning their daily duties, beginning with the ring of the rusty cow bell in the predawn hours of the day. Though Josiah must be nearing his eightieth year, he was efficient to a fault, his work unflagging, the grounds spotless, his trips to market with the trucking goods quick and successful.

Grace looked up and around the twenty-foot ceilings and walls. Now the most magnificent mansion for miles around, built of the best pine and yellow poplar, was hers. All hers. Inside lay costly rugs throughout with two large parlors filled with oil paintings decorating the walls. The kitchen housed a massive fireplace and walls of closets for their very best china.

Grace remembered the exact moment she broke the news of her father's death to the Thatchers. She ordered Josiah to ring the bell three times, a signal for the cabins to empty at once and for its inhabitants to gather near the giant oak that sat along the property line separating their dwellings from hers.

"My father—your master—Gilbert Henry Harrison has passed. It is I you will answer to now."

She recalled her feelings of power, how her voice demanded respect in its every inflection, how she heard it tremble only inwardly. She demanded it from the outset. This demand seemed unheard or unacknowledged as the immediate sadness of the moment caused great distress in the assemblage. Her father was kind, humble, a considerate man and a fair Master to the Thatchers. A good Master.

Eliza, Martha, Rose and Selena bowed their heads, small utterances escaping their lips. Ephriam rolled his eyes upwards as if to wish her father speedy delivery to Heaven. Master Gilbert had always bestowed kindness upon his laborers. He often called Ephriam to the main house and gave him a bucket of fresh roasted pork to distribute to his family. It was a treat, a welcomed diversion from the usual meals of hog fat, rice and vegetables.

Ephriam Thatcher towered almost a foot over his Master Gilbert. He was burly and muscular, his upper arms thick and knotted with veins from the days working in the fields. Though his body was tough and hard, his eyes were as soft and large as his master's, and held the same enduring gaze. Grace often commented to her father how Ephriam looked directly into his eyes and asked him why he permitted it. He would just smile dimly, sadly it seemed. Grace knew even at a young age how there was a direct communication—man-to-man, as if between equals, as if her father were letting Ephriam know how sorry he was for the state of things in these tempestuous times.

Grace knew how grateful the Thatchers were that they had landed on this plantation, under Master Gilbert's rule. Everyone knew all around them there were break-ups of families through sales of slaves. When Ephriam was sold to Gilbert for five hundred dollars, he begged Gilbert to make his next sales those of his wife, Martha, and their daughters Rose and Selena. Gilbert obliged and Ephriam suppressed a cry of joy when his brother Eliza, Mary and their children followed. Over the next year, a dozen Thatchers came to live on the Harrison plantation, including the baby Prudence who was born to Eliza and Mary just months later.

When the Mistress Grace took over, a feeling of uncertainty swept through the Thatchers. They knew her only for her cold and distant nature. Never a smile. Nor a kind word uttered.

She knew each of their names, but never addressed them, much less in their given names. Instead, she waved her bony index finger in their direction—an order—a direction of her thought in passing. A point of her finger or the flick of her hand was all that she used to communicate. The rest was done by Josiah, relating to them, her wishes conveyed second-hand.

Each week after her father's passing Grace called an early morning meeting under the great Oak tree. Josiah rang the rusty cow bell three times with such force, that thousands of startled black birds rose up from the nearby rice fields. As the weeks turned to months, the list of the Mistress's demands lengthened. Privileges dwindled accordingly.

"This week due to the shortage of chickens, dinner rations will be cut," she declared one week, pretending not to notice

Josiah's eyes meeting Ephriam's, their mutual scoff all the more obvious to her for their stoic and solemn faces.

Grace knew that for weeks her people had subsisted on dry ground corn, peanuts and old grains, that it had been months since she'd sent over a chicken. She felt no guilt that the smells of dumplings, of wild turkey basted in vinegar and lard drifted over to them in the still air from her kitchen.

Rose and Selena cooked her meals which they served in the dining room where she sat at the head of a long cherry wood table covered with a fancy cloth. The girls had to wait while Grace inspected each morsel of food on her plate. Only when she was completely satisfied did she dismiss them, allowing them to wait in the kitchen until she was done eating. They would then dutifully serve her desserts of fruit pies and tarts. Only after the last dish was cleaned and put away were they allowed to return to their cabin.

Most nights Martha was waiting supper for her girls, their dinners warming over the black hearth outside. After gobbling up their food, they would run to join the others down by the swamp creek that ran alongside their cabins. One by one the Thatchers would gather, every one hot, caked with dirt and bone-tired after toiling hours in the fields. Larkin, Rose and the others greeted one another, then stood on the short embankment that led into the water. Ephriam would enter first, immersing himself, letting the water wash the day's dust, cleansing his body and mind, then coming up for air, whooping and hollering, shaking his head back and forth.

The rest of the family would follow suit. As they slipped into the water, Ephriam would scramble back out to sit down at the trunk of a cypress tree, where he picked up his old guitar and positioned it on his knee. His treasured possession was chipped, its paint cracked, its strings often broken. With swollen, cut-up fingers he strummed, deep rich chords that quieted the weary souls before him.

Ephriam's songs were songs of freedom, about one day following the swamp creek down to the reaches of the Atlantic and heading out towards the horizon—confronting a line of peach-colored sky poised upon blue waters. He would nod to Mary, swaying waist deep in the creek, she grasping Martha's hand, then Martha holding onto Larkin and the circle would close. One by one the human circle grew larger until Baby Prudence was lifted up on to Eliza's shoulders where she squealed and gurgled.

After this cleansing Eliza led the evening prayer, giving thanks for their lives together and for their hope of liberty. Prayers then gave way to song—then laughter—as they chattered about the day's passing.

The Thatchers shared their nights at the water not only with themselves, but with other creatures. All around them there was movement—a heron stalking crayfish, lizards slithering about the rocks, bats overhead fluttering through the hickory trees towering over the blackwater stream.

And each night their joyous voices carried through the trees, drifting over the Harrison estate. Grace, dabbing her face in the sitting room, heard them. And every night, she bristled, feeling as if they were invading her thoughts, the main one being the question, "What is it about those waters that can provoke such gaiety in a person?"

She knew they live in cramped dwellings, wore tattered clothes, ate chicken scratchings. Yet, by night they seemed to have new breath—vigorous power to rise above it all and rejoice.

"What's in that water you bathe in at night?" she asked Selena one afternoon in the kitchen. The girl avoided her eyes as she continued lining trays with wild plums and whortleberries for drying in the sun.

Selena shrugged.

"Is there a potion?" Grace asked impatiently, her foot tapping, her arms folded.

"No, Ma'am."

"A spell?"

"No, Ma'am." The girl did not flinch, and kept her eye on the tray of fruits. "Is there something in your water that I haven't seen here?"

"Yes, Ma'am," Selena said wistfully, suddenly.

"Now what would that be?"

"Diamonds, Ma'am."

Grace pressed her bony finger down hard on the girl's shoulder. "Did you say diamonds?"

"Yes, Ma'am. On the warm, warm water. Hundreds of 'em."

Grace clicked her tongue. She shook her head. "Warm water from a chilly swamp stream and it's loaded with diamonds!" She lifted Selena's head from her task sensing a teasing smile. It had disappeared.

The next night Grace waited until midnight. It was still and humid outdoors, the only noise came from the high-pitched screech of a baby Barred Owl. Grace paced the floor of her bedroom. She ran her hand along the smooth wood of her dressing table, touching the hairbrush and assortment of ribbons and bows. She smoothed a wrinkle from the blanket that lay folded at the end of her bed, checking for new folds or creases. Everything was perfect — clean and in its place.

Grace sat at the edge of her bed. She thought about the skittish silly girl Selena and felt that beneath her expressionless eyes, the girl was laughing at her. The girl had never even snickered or talked back to her in a mocking tone. Yet, Grace felt it was there, right beneath the surface. It baffled her, for she felt that she could never reach the Thatchers, never truly have complete control. They gave her the respect she demanded. They never complained or rebelled in any way. But she could not infiltrate their spirit. This angered her even more.

How she detested their evening gatherings, their intimate chorus cutting through the night mist, on its nomadic journey to her lonely quarters, to her ears. Even in the late autumn months, when the frost clung to the trees, the Thatchers would gather.

With this thought Grace's thin frame shivered. She wondered how someone could stand in dismal waters and gather enough strength at the end of the day to exhale a song.

Even in times of sickness, when the baby Prudence was burning up with fever, they took her down to the creek. Grace overheard Selena and Rose talking in the kitchen about how Ephriam held the child in the murky liquid until it covered her little body. The baby whimpered weakly under his mellow words and his soothing touch and the family formed a circle around them chanting and praying. This time there was no blissful chorus, only words of asking to bring the dear child back to health. The very next evening Grace heard their voices—not grievous but jubilant once again.

"The baby Prudence?" Grace inquired the following day. She had to know.

"No more fever, Ma'am."

Grace sniffed. She turned away on her heel and never mentioned the baby by name again. But that night she sat at her desk and wrote another entry in her journal.

"I must see for myself this divine rhythm that runs through the stream. A rhythm that is buoyant over trouble and hardship, that rises above sickness and keeps the weary heart beating. I must know for myself what blows gusts of renewed energy into each and every bone-weary soul."

Grace Harrison

August 30, 1832

Grace slipped quietly out of the house, her ears primed for Josiah who sometimes wandered the grounds late at night. She didn't want to be seen. She crept across the property to the stream behind her house and stood staring down at the water. Off came her nightgown, and night cap, then slippers. Clad in just her cotton chemise undergarment, she entered the water, walking further in until it came to her knees. It was cold, ice cold, and Grace shivered in the August night. A turtle basking on a log nearby eyed her. She turned away from its beady eyes, embarrassed suddenly, feeling her face color.

Reflecting on the water under the moon's glare was the image of a large Bald Cypress, where she saw markings in the full moon of Red-Bellied woodpeckers.

She took two steps deeper into the water and stood waiting with her hands on her hips. "Why, it's just a spot of cold, dirty water. Nothing more," she whispered angrily.

She waited for the water to turn warm—for the urge to laugh or to break into song. "Who would want to sing standing in this muck?"

She crawled back on to the embankment, grabbed her robe and ran back to the house.

After that night, Grace's moods darkened. Each day there was a new rule from her delivered by Josiah: No praying out loud in the morning, report to work one hour earlier, no singing in the fields at noon. Still each evening she sat alone by the window, hating the voices that made their way to her.

She began to take these increasingly blacker moods out on Selena and Rose. When the girls dutifully chopped vegetables and peeled potatoes, Grace carped, never satisfied. She made them stay longer hours, sometimes long after she had finished eating and the dishes were done and put away. She knew from the rumblings of their stomachs that they were hungry, yet not a flicker of agitation crossed their faces. When Grace finally released them, they ran out the door, across the dark fields to their own meal of hog fat and rice that Martha had kept warm.

"Today is my birthday. I miss you Father. I am wearing the fine dress you bought me last year. The lavender silk dress with the puffed sleeves and handsome matching bonnet. You were so healthy then. Strong. I will celebrate alone this year, wearing this dress in your honor. Your catching smile and sparkling eyes will be with me today and always."

Grace

September 10, 1832

When Gilbert Harrison was alive, Grace's birthday was a day of celebration, a day on which he indulged her, presenting her with gifts throughout the day such as baskets of chocolates from Charleston, dresses and shoes with fancy ornaments. This year it was raining. Dark clouds hung low outside steaming windows as lightning crackled across the sky. No celebration.

"Another day's work lost," Grace muttered, for the storm brought not only rain but pelting hail stones that bounced about after hitting the ground.

She sat, adorned in her lavender dress, her bonnet tied securely under her chin, and watching the raindrops stick against the glass. She dozed until the faint sound of a guitar woke her, its reverberating tune comforting her in her isolation. Ephriam's voice penetrated through the rain, his song a call to his Poppa, whose spirit he beckoned. Grace listened carefully to the lyrics, telling of good folks in the world, folks pressing for freedom for all mankind. Larkin's voice accompanied Ephriam's wail. She heard the sounds of Josiah's labors, cleaning a back room of the main house, cease.

" Just round the corner, Poppa" Ephriam sang. "Just round the corner."

Grace closed her eyes, listening to the haunting voices. She dozed again, her last vision a drop of rain inching its way down the window, matching the single tear drop that slid down the sleeping woman's cheek.

As if spurred by her birthday song, each night following, Grace slipped out into the night and go to the blackwater stream. There she would stand waist-deep in the water and wait for the spell to come to her. It never came. The only sounds she heard was the rustling of warblers nesting deep in the hollows and the croak of the frog that watched with amusement at the lady shivering in her undergarments.

Grace could stand it no longer. At the next meeting she marched haughtily to the oak tree and announced a new rule. This time she delivered it herself.

"Tonight, there will be no gathering at the waters. All washings will be done using water from the well on the south side of the property."

This time the message drew a reaction. Ephriam raised his eyebrows in question. Quick looks flittered about and Grace caught Martha's frown. Yet, no one dared to question.

That night, Grace left her house and marched across the fields towards the cabin compound. The moon was full and bright. It helped lead the way for the Mistress as she made her way to the magical waters. Twigs crunched under her feet, tearing into her satin slippers. Peering through the trees she saw the tiny overcrowded shacks, the doors ajar to let in the night's air. She saw Mary holding the baby Prudence who was fussing. She heard Eliza and Larkin conversing loudly.

Grace crept down through the thicket. She stood at the embankment and took off her robe, ignoring the night autumn air, brisk with the hint of early winter. She inched into the water and slowly waded forward a few steps. She looked at the surroundings, the forest dense with branches that formed a dark wall where night birds hid, chirping in the darkness. A hawk flew across the swamp stream and the rustle of wings startled her. She heard a branch crack and jumped. Her heart pounded wildly in her chest.

Suddenly she felt vulnerable, petrified of lethal swamp snakes, or that she could trip and almost drown and no one would hear her cries for help. Her fright froze her, her arms heavy lead pipes hanging at her sides.

Another branch crackled. She knew she was not alone. A pair of eyes appeared from behind a tree and Grace shrieked into the frosty air. Then, she stopped. It was the face of Selena.

"Selena!" Grace whispered, one of the few times she called the girl by name. Selena skirted down the embankment. Fully clothed, she slipped into the water with her Mistress.

"Selena...help me. I can't move."

Selena waded forward, the water rising higher on her shorter frame until it reached her neck. Yet she continued and then held out her hand. Grace's heaviness of limb seemed to dissolve by degrees and she managed to grab the hand of the child and hold on tightly.

Grace took a step forward but tripped and fell into the water, submerged. When she popped up through the surface she sputtered and shook her face, trying to clear her eyes. Selena still held on to her hand and pulled her in close. Grace stomped her foot in frustration but the once-powerful gesture was now nothing more than a swish through the bottom of murky water.

Selena could not hold back a minute longer. The sight of her Mistress in her undergarments, her hair drenched and wild about her shoulders—stomping her feet with authority was too much. A squeal of laughter escaped. The young girl's body shook and tears rolled from her eyes. Grace stared back reproachful, yet never let go of the girl's hand.

Then, Grace felt the beginning of a smile. Her pierced lips began to quiver and a giggle escaped her lips. Soon the two stood howling in the darkness when Selena, in a daring move, cupped her hands and sent a splash of water into Grace's face. Startled, Grace returned the gesture.

So taken by the moment neither saw the others appearing from behind the trees. Ephriam stepped out first, clutching his guitar. He sat down on the ground at his usual place while the rest of the Thatcher family boldly slipped into the water, against the wishes of the Mistress Harrison, who was too busy giggling and slapping water in her young charge's face.

Ephriam began to strum a deep, resonating tune. Rose reached out and took Grace's other hand. Martha, Eliza and the others grasped hands and formed a circle under the glare of the full September moon. Grace tried to speak but stopped before the words left her mouth. She was struck dumb by all that lay before her.

The moon's light reflected across the night water causing masses of diamond-like drops to lay across the wet glass. Water lilies floated near the edges and a sweet fragrance of dried wild orchids drifted by.

"Like the Garden of Eden," she thought.

The human circle swayed back and forth chanting and singing. Grace looked at each of the family, her family, as if studying them for the first time. She saw handsome faces, earnest and forgiving. She realized at that very moment it was not a spell lying about these waters. It was not warmer here or more beautiful than the stream that ran near her home.

It was the nourishment of the human touch — the sharing of love and spirit between one and other that made these waters rich. It was a bond of forgiveness — of caring — that welcomed in its fold each and every child of the universe.

The swamp waters rippled against the gentle forces of swaying. A sweet medley of voices lifted high above the thicket of pine and hickory and traveled down the stream. This night...Grace's voice was among them, her song bellowed from the depths of her heart. Just released from the shackles of loneliness, she held on tight to her new freedom and to the open arms that embraced her.

The same full moon shone over everyone that night.

Lifeline

Briarwood was a sleepy town without fast food restaurants or traffic signs. Its dusty roads were flanked with rows of weeping willows, its lakeshore speckled with weather-beaten cottages whose yards backed up to an old railroad line, where nightly a freight trains' whistle soloed as it bound down the tracks. Along the shoreline was Zeke's Marina, filled with a motley assortment of boats, most still under the shrink-wraps that kept them covered during the colder months.

Briarwood was also home to thirteen-year-old Mortimer Montgomery whom most considered good-natured, thoughtful, and well mannered. But thirteen being an awkward age for most boys, Mortimer was no exception. Always chubby, as he grew his weight flourished: "fat" was the word others used to describe him. As if this weren't enough, he had pimples, and a voice that forsook him at odd moments, rising an octave and cracking in mid-sentence when he tried to speak. But it wasn't the excess weight that bothered him, nor even his bad skin or his unreliable voice. It was his name: Mortimer Mathias Montgomery.

"Couldn't you have picked Tom? Or Joe? Even Pete?" he would ask his parents. "What were you thinking?"

But he knew the answer before they spoke. "It was your grandfather's name. You should feel honored to carry on the legacy."

An honor? He laughed. It was more like a curse, a headache that he was forced to endure each day of his life. His name was infamous. Didn't the girls at school use it as a jingle when they jumped rope? Didn't his teacher relish Mortimer rolling off her tongue to a chorus of snickers? It seemed to her a cause for celebration, a favorite task, he knew. She did not address him when the class was distracted by noise or shuffling feet, nor when the pencil sharpener spit out pieces of lead and wood, nor when outside traffic filtered through the windows. No, his teacher waited for silence, when the classroom was as quiet as Sunday morning.

Only at such moments, when no conversation broke the still, did his teacher speak his name. And she would take her time, making sure it was heard at the far end of the room. She would enunciate each vowel, each consonant, breaking it into paragraphs so it would last longer..."Mor–ti–mer...Ma–thai–is Mont--go-- mery."

He remembered the time he approached her politely when school began. "If it would be okay, I would like you to call me Mort," he requested.

It was not too much to ask, he figured. She called Bartholomew, Bart and Christopher, Chris. But it was not so simple then as Mortimer watched her blow her nose in a square linen handkerchief and stand there as if expecting him to plunk an apple down on her desk. He shuffled his feet, wondering if she even heard him, and watched her pale green beady eyes stare off into space. Maybe she was contemplating what to make for dinner, he thought, or watching the paint dry on the wall. When she looked back down at him, he seemed to her an afterthought.

"Thank you, Mortimer, you may sit down," she said.

The sound of his name that day was inevitably followed by what would become the interminable snickering. And this chorus from the beginning was led by Bobby Ray, his number one enemy. His bully. Mortimer hated everything about Bobby Ray, his tough looks, his height, his muscles. His perfectly combed blond hair even bugged Mortimer, like a giant wave dipping across the top of his head. But it wasn't his looks or his hair that terrified Mortimer. It was that Bobby Ray's word was law, especially to his gang of followers, the "Six Pack"–with Bobby Ray, Butch, Andy, Vic, Spike, and Art.

And Bobby Ray took the greatest pleasure in tormenting Mortimer, hounding him from the moment he arrived at school until the last ring of the bell. There was no escaping. Even during the summer months, while shooting marbles or riding bikes at dusk, Bobby Ray and his friends would shadow him. Mortimer had resigned himself to the belittling. He never retaliated. They called him stupid. They called him fat. Once he looked at them, shielded by the invisible armor he had long ago adopted and asked, "Could you call me Mort?"

It would be a sign of respect, he felt. It meant little to them but everything to him. "Mort"... the word was blunt- it could be uttered in the hallway in passing... it could be spoken in a gathering along with others, without being pulled back and dissected. And it ended abruptly. Like Clark and Pat.

His request was met with snickers.

In the town of Briarwood there were no theaters, no dairy queens or drive-in hamburger stands around which the young people could congregate. In the summer time, on hot afternoons, everyone flocked to the lake. The lake was small, set off by pockets of inlets and coves, and supported by steep jagged inclines, perfect for climbing and diving.

Every summer Bobby Ray and the Six Pack would be loud and obnoxious, and claim one end of the lake as their domain. And the gang would screech, "Mortimer," during lulls in their territorial terrorism. And he would bear the misfortune of hearing it four more times as an echo, bouncing off the wall of rocks. Mortimer would keep his distance, always sitting off to the side, far enough away from their reaches. Yet their calls never forgot to remind him what he already knew... Mortimer Montgomery could not swim.

"It's because someone your size can't stay above water," they taunted. "You'd sink to the bottom," Bobby Ray would begin, then Vic and soon all the six pack would be joining in.

Mortimer would watch them from a safe distance. He was used to their jeers. He had no clever comeback, no real defense, since it was true. Everyone knew Mortimer waded in water that only reached his knees. It was a brave day when he ventured out further. The thought of tripping and falling under the water made him cringe.

Mortimer wished he had the courage to swim. But there was something spooky about the water, he thought. Always had been, even when he was younger and his parents took him to the lake for a family picnic. He remembered that within minutes his younger brothers and cousins ran full force into the water, then splashed and dunked each other under, sputtering when they broke the surface, laughing at the fun of it all. But he always watched from the sidelines. "Mortimer's a baby!" the younger kids would yell at him.

He wouldn't flinch, but merely stayed safely up on the sand, fearing that if his family chose, they could have converged on him, using their strength and dragged him out to the water. Instead, he would sit on his security blanket, inched up almost to the grass, where he was safe. That way, Mortimer could turn and run the other way. It was in those younger days that Mortimer started wearing a whistle around his neck — a huge silver whistle dangling on a thin red rope.

People would ask why he wore it, to which he would invariably reply, "To call my dog." The truth was Mortimer's stone-deaf dog couldn't hear the shriek of a whistle if it was blown an inch from his ear. And the old hound never ventured more than a few feet from their house. No, Mortimer Montgomery wore the whistle for protection–for the time some kids might, as a laugh, pull him into the water He thought it would alert adults that there was trouble. That Mortimer needed rescuing, that he was submerged in the dirty lake and sinking.

At the lake, Mortimer usually sat alone. Squinting his eyes in another direction, he would surreptitiously watch the Six Pack. Butch was the best swimmer. He would stand on the rocky ledge above the deep part of the lake and wait until he knew he had an audience. Then up came his arms positioned like darts on each side of his head. He stared at the spot in the water he wanted to hit and with a short jumping motion took off, arching through the air. "Way to go!" The accolades came, the cheers starting before he hit the water. And Butch would swim to shore and go through the routine of being patted on the back.

Then Vic would scale the rocks to the rope-swing that dangled out on a sturdy branch. He would swing out over the deep end, jump and pretend he was drowning, yelling for help. The others would pretend not to hear. It was a game they played trying to see if Mortimer would make a move to the water. It seemed as if it were a test, that the Six Pack wondered if Mortimer had the stuff to react, if it were serious enough, if he would forget his fear.

He watched Vic now, at it once again, flailing his arms and going under for almost two minutes. Mortimer was tired of the game. they had tried it so many times before. He sat on the sand and waited for Vic to come up through the surface. But this time, as the seconds passed, Mortimer began to sweat, fidgeted, and scratched his head, coughing. Enough already, he thought, I know you can swim. I'm not going out there to drown, knowing this is a joke.

He imagined himself wading out over his head, sinking, his nose and mouth filling with dirty lake water. Lost in his musings, he found himself up on his feet and peering out at the circle where Vic went down. As loud as he could muster, he yelled across to the six pack, "Your friend is in trouble!"

They turned their backs, talking among themselves without acknowledging Mortimer's calls. He blew the whistle, the screech hurt his ears. Mortimer started to whimper. He walked in circles not knowing what to do. Someone was at the bottom of the lake, drowning before his eyes. It wouldn't take much to paddle out there and save him. But his fear grounded him.

Then, he heard a splash and saw Vic's head surface. He heard spitting and sputtering,...followed by a chorus of snickering, "Mortimer...Montgomery!" They enjoyed calling his name, like he was some clown in town for their amusement. He knew he had been had. Again. Once and always, a fool. By now he should have known. It wasn't the first time they had done this. It wouldn't be the last.

The next time it would be different, Mortimer vowed. He would sit stone-faced, not moving a muscle. He would wait three, four, five minutes if he had to and would hum every tune he knew. He envisioned one of them sitting at the bottom, holding their breath until bursting...wanting to tug the last ounce of fear from him.

He would not even look. Instead, he would carve his name in the sand with a stick, sitting backwards to their glares. Maybe an ambulance would have to come. Reporters, detectives. They would have to call themselves the "Five Pack". And all because they wanted to see him squirm. Their names would be in the papers. He gloated over the headlines, "Five guys allow their best friend to drown."

"My name is MORT!" he yelled back, but they were gone.

It wasn't long before the Dog Days of summer arrived. Long days towards the end of August with their sleepy stretches of hot afternoons, days of hundred-degree sticky humid air hanging thick over idle baseball fields and surrounding acres of mulch and dust. On such days even the hollows were crammed with wildlife, quail, squirrels and raccoons, insulating themselves from the sweltering sun.

On one Sunday afternoon Mortimer laid out his lunch on the ground at the far side of the shore, sitting cross-legged, in a quiet place shaded by trees. It was silent, but for a gentle hiss of wind through the grass. He liked it when no one was around.

Methodically, he smoothed out his napkin on his lap and arranged the items for his lunch–a jelly sandwich, carton of milk, and a slice of chocolate cake. He began munching on his sandwich and slurping milk and watched as a line of ants join him, marching in a circle around his food. Mortimer brushed them away with one hand, his jelly-smeared hand still held the sticky bread in the other. It was cool under the tree. He was relaxed and focused on a ladybug that was crawling up a twig. He looked closer at her red back and tried to count the spots, but his shadow spooked her. She flew away, buzzing past his nose.

He wished it were always like this. A noiseless afternoon. The lake water did not even look threatening. Today it was calm, a deep green color, flat and glassy. Something startled him and he turned. He looked off to the other side near the cover and saw Bobby Ray. What's he doing here alone, he wondered, without the Six Pack? Bobby Ray never traveled anywhere without the other five by his side.

Mortimer crept in closer to get a better look. He watched quietly as the boy scaled the side of the rocks on to the overhanging tree branch until he reached the rope-tire. Then he balanced on the tire, moving inches ahead, pushing behind until he gained momentum.

Mortimer thought he looked strange, something was different, he didn't know what it was. Then, it came to him: Mortimer realized that alone, Bobby Ray moved differently. He wasn't swaggering. His face didn't have a sneer. He looked like...well, a regular guy.

Mortimer knew that Bobby Ray thought he was alone. The bully whooped and hollered and sang the Star-Spangled Banner, listening to his voice bounce off the wall of rocks around him. He swung the tire back and forth out farther over the water. Mortimer continued watching him, his curiosity deepening. He wasn't acting wild like the others; he didn't look like Tarzan flying confidently through the air. Instead, Bobby Ray pitched and rolled, cautiously, as if testing the waters–as if testing his courage before jumping.

As he gained momentum, the rope-tire swung outward. Mortimer saw he was getting ready to leap. A minute later he did, landing farther out than any of them ever had as long as Mortimer could remember, crashing through the water with a huge splash. Mortimer stood and watched as the boy thrashed about under the water's surface as if stunned. He rose and was fearful suddenly as Bobby Ray surfaced. His feet were not able to touch the bottom.

"So, swim," Mortimer yelled out. "Swim to shore."

Bobby Ray caught sight of him and tried to wave. His body sunk with each attempt.

"Not this time. Not another hoax," Mortimer whispered as he watched Bobby Ray sputter and shake his head, as if pleading. He kept going down, coming up, like the same old game. Mortimer tried to turn his back, thinking they just wanted to see his worried face and doubtful eyes. He knew Bobby Ray would tell them everything. Every detail. Maybe they were here already, hiding behind the trees. He listened for snickering. He heard nothing.

The seconds seemed like hours to Mortimer, noticing Bobby Ray staying down for longer intervals of time. How many more of these games do they want to play? Why can't they move on to someone else? He wondered who would be the next person they would torment if he were not around. He knew he was an easy target. Everything he felt they read on his face. He needed to become stronger, to fight back. To scream at them angrily and not stand for their endless cruelty.

It was time to teach them a lesson. If he didn't do it now, the torment would continue. Turning his back on Bobby Ray was easy; listening to him sputtering, crying for help was not. He's really doing a good job of acting, Mortimer thought as he started to fidget, scratch his head and hum a tune, the Happy Birthday song. He started to cough—a nervous, dry hack.

Doubt crept in. A thought ignited, making him shake his head in doubt.

Could it be possible that Bobby Ray didn't know how to swim? He thought back to the times he saw the Six Pack out in the water. Andy could swim backwards. Butch could dive. Art, Spike and Vic were always fooling around in the deep end. He searched his memory. It seemed incredible but he simply could not recall Bobby Ray out in the water. He was the one who stayed on shore, climbing rocks and yelling the loudest at Mortimer. His taunting, his name calling was the loudest and most cruel. But, yes, Mortimer recalled, he always did it from the sidelines: the leader never swam out to meet the rest.

The game had taken a wicked turn. Mortimer realized his power. No one was around. God's will would be done in just a few minutes, with his back turned to the bully, ignoring his desperate pleas, not a classmate, not a bird, not even a ladybug to witness.

By doing nothing, he could end it all: the name calling, ridicule, humiliation. Without Bobby Ray the others would go about their business. It was always his lead they followed. Did he have it in him? Could he live his life knowing he had turned his back on a dying kid? Maybe.

He heard his name called. But this time it was different. He jerked his body, turning to the direction of the bobbing head. His ears perked, wondering if they had heard it right.

"Mort!"

Bobby Ray was calling him. Finally. Finally, Bobby Ray was using the name HE commanded, not that gave the guy amusing material to work with through the day. Years vanished in those seconds, gone was the memory of the name the bully could never let roll off his lips. It was a sign; it was surrender, capitulation. It was acknowledgment: four letters ended a lifetime of hell.

Mortimer scrambled to the top of the hill. Breathless, sweating, he reached out to the outstretched tree limb and tore at the knot, trying to release the tire. He clawed at the knot loosening the thick rope, his knuckles scraped from the abrasions. Finally, the tire came loose. Mortimer aimed, then hurled it far out to Bobby Ray below, whose voice was now feeble. The throw was on target. Weary arms grasped at the rubber tire, and clung to it with diminishing strength.

He slid down the hill and stood at the water's edge. There was no time to wait. Bobby Ray was exhausted, his last bit of strength squandered. Twice Mortimer saw him slip under the tire. He grabbed the whistle around his neck and blew. But no one could hear it, he realized. They were alone. Pulling off his socks and shoes, he walked fully clothed into the lake. It was his nightmare visiting him on a Sunday afternoon.

The water came to his knees, then up to his waist. Still, he pushed forward until his feet left the bottom. Then, with renewed strength, he began kicking and paddling like he saw the younger children do. It kept him buoyant.

Mortimer flopped his ankles up and down, spitting out water that was filling his mouth, all the while keeping his eyes glued to Bobby Ray. He finally reached him and the tire, which he also grabbed, gasping for breath. He positioned Bobby Ray's arms back firmly on to the tire. With every ounce of strength, he plunged ahead, forward towards shore. Kicking, lurching, pulling the tire and the boy, he made headway, only inches at a time. Mortimer's bulky form bobbed up and down through the water like a seal.

When they reached ground, both boys clawed their way up on to the sand and collapsed. They lay exhausted, choking and rasping, then pulled themselves up trying to appear calm and assembled in front of each other. Neither spoke. There was too much to say. And nothing. What happened was something that would be kept between the two of them, Mortimer knew. A secret, locked away forever. And Mortimer held the key.

Humble, yet gallant in the same moment, a mutual respect arose between them.

Bobby Ray broke the silence. "Thanks, Mort."

Bobby Ray repeated the name, then shrugged his shoulders because he couldn't find words to follow. Mortimer stood, looking down at his former bully, at his pale face, his soaked hair flat and matted and wondered why he had ever feared him.

Then, he took the whistle from his neck. He bent down and placed it around the neck of Bobby Ray, who looked at him, dumbfounded. Mortimer walked away, back to the shade tree to finish his jelly sandwich.

Her Majesty

Queen Isabel was a wise and kind ruler. She reigned over her kingdom alone for her husband had been dead many years. Her castle was a grand beauty. It was her treasure, a glistening palace that stood tall in the summer sun. The castle was admired by everyone who saw it, because it had so many towers, a grand drawbridge, and a courtyard where joyous celebrations were held. There was always an air of festivity outside the castle, with music and storytellers and jesters. Isabel laughed heartily at the jesters, in pompoms and bells as they juggled colorful bottles and danced around her. She clapped and joined in song with others in folly, while overseeing sumptuous feasts of pheasant, fruits and cheeses.

The queen was loved by everyone because she was a generous soul. Whether she spoke with nobles or common peasants, all were considered equal in the queen's eyes. She did not wear a grand tiara on her head. Her gowns were not made of silk or taffeta, only of plain coarse wool. Her majesty did not even sit on a high throne, but walked alongside her people, listening to their troubles and their dreams.

She was kind not only to her servants but to all who were less fortunate than she. Those who worked for the queen never went cold, for she provided them with warm clothes to wear. They never went hungry, for she gave them plenty of food to eat.

The queen was not even aware of the admiration she aroused. There was a mysterious fascination about how someone who held such great power could be so giving to those who had so little. What made her welcome all with such love and acceptance? they pondered. No one knew the answer. But they felt fortunate to revel in her compassion.

Each day there would be a knock at the castle door. Families from around the countryside stood before the queen. She knew from the glimmering depths of their eyes that they were hungry. She would receive her guests with welcome arms. "Take this bread," she would tell them. Each guest left with fresh warm bread from the oven. They were bade a tender farewell. The queen was at peace when she knew all around her were fed. Only then could she sleep with a full heart.

Although she ruled with honesty, the queen kept a secret that she share with no one. She grew sad when the day ended and the sun started falling from the sky. It was during this time that a great shadow stood over her castle, casting a haunting gloom overhead. The queen grew quiet because the appearance of the shadow meant an end to her joyous day.

But alas, she was unable to hold back the hours, to block the day's demise. Over time, Isabel learned to acknowledge the coming darkness with wistful acceptance. She knew when it was time for one last song, and although she sang the morning's bright tune it carried a lilt of forlorn and despair.

And so the sun set on yet another glorious day. The early evening air was balmy and sweet. The looming shadow appeared...the voice — its tone filled with understanding greeted the queen. "It's time to go, Isabel," the shadow spoke. She looked up into the kind eyes of the officer. He bent down and brushed sand from her dirty face and hair. Officer O'Riley stood, waiting. His gold badge, his baton, was a familiar sight to the grand lady. "Beach is closing," he prodded. "Nice," he told her, standing back and admiring the great castle that stood in the sand. He noted the many towers, the gatehouse, and even a drawbridge that was built around a moat of seawater.

Last minute stragglers on the New York beach came to admire the structure before leaving. Children squealed their delight, their parents nodded approval, but out of respect, no one dared touch the woman's treasured palace.

The officer helped her to her feet and watched as Isabel shuffled her weary body across the sand. He shook his head, watching her limp home... back to her cardboard box in the alleyway. Once there, she was acknowledged by her friends, that sat around her on the sidewalk, resting their aching backs against the building's brick wall. Tired, hungry faces stared back at her.

Isabel reached deep into the pocket of her tattered robe and took out a chunk of bread. She broke off pieces and handed it to the glimmering eyes that spoke. Not until the last morsel of bread was gone, could she rest. Then, she settled in her tiny domain. On her stone pillow the queen slept with a full heart. She dreamt of her castle. There were sumptuous feasts, tables of pheasants, fruits and cheese. In her dream she clapped and sang and court jesters danced and juggled around her.

At the beach, the night tide reached shore. It tugged the castle back to the sea with each forceful wave. The walls and towers crumbled. Piece by piece the palace broke apart, then was pulled in where it lay scattered about on the ocean's floor. In just a few hours the queen's castle was gone. But the granules that lay at the bottom of the sea sparkled under the moonlight like jewels, as they would for all eternity. Because they were royal gems — built on a dream. And touched by greatness.

Eagle Lake

Red-faced and puffing and out of breath, Abe capitulated to the clouds of gnats swarming around his face. They just kept coming, undaunted and unaffected. How he longed to simply raise his hand and swat away the pesky insects, but his arms lay limp, still folded primly in his lap, in the same pose his son Thomas no doubt believed befitted a stroke survivor. He felt no less helpless now than he had two years ago when he suffered his stroke. Just as helpless, just as immobile, so much so that for two summers running he had been strapped into his chair on the family's pontoon boat cruising Eagle Lake.

And like last summer his children and grandchildren generally ignored him, talking around him as if he were a shadow on the deck. Abe wanted to join them as he used to, telling them jokes and reading them stories.

This was not how it was supposed to end for seventy-year-old recently retired lawyer, Abe thought, especially one who had led such a productive professional life. The Silver Fox, they called him, clever in and out of the courtroom, his white thick wavy hair his trademark, his burly frame carried tall and with dignity, his deeply bronzed skin from his summers on the lake a year-round phenomenon which carried long into the sunless Minnesota winter months.

When his wife, Miriam, passed away, Abe was devastated. Two years went by before he learned how to smile again. Soon after his smile returned, he found himself looking at women, and started back into circulation after a forty-year hiatus. The future looked promising. And once again he was working full throttle, picking up his phone, filling his calendar pages, accepting invitations from long-ignored friends who had stuck by him. Then he was struck down.

The stroke seemed to come out of nowhere. One morning while reading the paper a strange rush of blood flooded over his face and he felt hot. Putting down the paper, he tried to get up to allay the sudden dizziness. He could not get up. A strange weight kept him fixed in the chair, the weight of his own body, he realized, suddenly acting like it didn't own him. The same body that once supported his brawny frame with such bearing and dignity became lifeless and uncooperative. Abe felt betrayed. It was as if some cruel prankster had taken over, to undermine Abe's love of life, and his pride. In seconds his life was pulled from him out from under. His resulting feebleness enraged him, seemingly more for his inability to do the simple things like patting a friend on the back, or filling his favorite pipe with cherry tobacco, or gathering his grandchildren into his arms. Or hugging them.

Small favors that his razor-sharp mind was still intact, since no one seemed to notice, or care. Besides, he could not talk, his mouth disowned him as well. His mind was alive, swirling with songs he had left to sing, and politics to discuss— words with meaning—but what good were they when they came out garbled. And when he ventured to say something, anything, some people would look away, embarrassed perhaps, and would pretend not to hear. Others feigned politeness, as if they understood his words, though not trying to, then would answer him with patronizing irrelevancies, talking about things he never mentioned. They made no effort to understand him. His expressive baritone was effectively silenced by the prankster who had stolen his limbs. It hurt not to be understood.

Yet, his boys took care of his needs, and he was grateful. They found him a room in a pleasant nursing home with the medical attention he needed. Little did they know that the once-robust Abraham had now all but given up on life, that the strange remote quiet he had slipped into was not the result of his illness, but was his own choice.

This dormancy had become habitual, even on this balmy August afternoon on the lake. Judging by his family's lack of acknowledgment of him he must have appeared as invisible as he felt. Abe's frustration enraged him. Closing his eyes he saw himself standing tall and breaking his bindings, then demanding that his loved ones at least speak to him, look at him, not through him. After then cuffing their ears, he would climb up and take his rightful place in his Captain's chair, spool his shiny black rod and reel with a fresh line, and cast out on the water. Eagle Lake, he thought blissfully, prime waters, the best in the Minnesota for Walleye and Bass.

It was only fair, he thought, that he be master once again of his own boat, the "Blue Pontoon," handed down to him by his own father. Certainly, his family didn't value it. They used it only as a craft designed to cool off, to skim hurriedly across the waters, to pass the hours on a hot summer day. Sure, he thought, it wasn't the classiest of boats, but to him it was a million-dollar yacht. For years, he doted on it, washed it down once a week at the dock and periodically cleaned it, all seasons except winters when it was in storage. He polished the rusted railings and swept the deck and built cabinets to hold their life jackets and tackle boxes.

Lawyer be damned, he thought, eyes still closed, his love was the water. He was a tough, capable, crafty fisherman, the best. Before he became immobile that is. Dismissing this last thought, he saw himself once again in charge, sitting high and proud, filling his chair like a man — Chief Navigator, Captain, Skipper of his blue square vessel. He recalled the old days when his boys accompanied him every Saturday for a trip out on Eagle Lake. Mitch was only nine back then, Thomas two years younger. At the time his sons couldn't wait to scramble up on deck. Abe would help them assemble their rods and reels, bait their hooks with minnows, and make sure their bobbers were lined up evenly.

Abe could still hear their voices: "Poppa, will you help me respool this?" or "Poppa, will you put the Nightcrawler on the hook for me?" That Abe barely had time to fish himself didn't bother him at all. He savored their requests. Every few minutes the boys would call to him, tugging at his trousers, asking him for help. He loved hearing their shouts at the sights around the lake. "See the brown duck with babies!" — "Look at the rings moving around the bobber, is something biting?" Mitch and

Thomas would work as a team, he recalled. Abe would help them with their tackle, Mitch would hold the net, and Thomas would fill the buckets with their catch.

Every Saturday the boys would compete for the biggest fish. The day Abe pulled in a six-pound bass, he hid it from them, carefully putting it aside to show Miriam later. Saturdays were their days. He had lured in enough catches in his time. He lived to see their faces when the striped bobbers pulled under the surface and the line tugged in their hands. Whether it was a small trout or a fat catfish, the look on their faces were the same. Surprise, thrill, exhilaration.

Drenched, splattered with mud, they would hold up their catches proudly for their father to see, sometimes even the tiniest fish dangled at the end of the hook. "Throw him back," Abe told Mitch and Thomas when the catch was too small. "He's too little. Send him back to his momma."

And the afternoon hours would fly by, the boat drifting lazily across the lake. On the way they would pass by wind-swept beaches and rocks and people on the shore fishing, their eyes glued to their lines. As they passed by, Abe would yell in his baritone, and whip off and tip his sailor cap to the startled, then smiling, folks. They knew this big man's Eagle Lake greeting. Hats would wave back, and salutes and fish would materialize. Abe could still hear the laughter and greetings as the Blue Pontoon passed along the shores. That minute of recognition among fishermen meant more to Abe than winning any grand prize.

"You look like Popeye, not Poppa," was the boys' standard kid to Abe, who knew he did with his pipe and sailor hat. He would smile as Mitch and Thomas leaned out over the side of the boat to mimic his greetings, and hold up their line of fish for all on shore to see. Following his lead, they too would doff their caps and wave, eyes wide and faces red.

And as the day progressed, the buckets would fill to overflowing. Mouths would water. Miriam would be waiting, Abe and his boys knew. She would empty the vats of walleye and northern pike and clean them with a sharp knife, the scales flying about her. When the frying pan was sizzling with melted butter, she would fry up the fillets and they would fill their plates. On summer nights they ate outside on lawn chairs on the grass overlooking the lake. The boys would be done first and run off to play, but Miriam and Abe would sit longer, sipping coffee, watching the sun set over the misty bay.

Abe opened his eyes, memories melting away in the humidity. He looked at his boys, now grown men, sad that they had lost their love for the lake. They were caught up in their own lives, raising children and trying to get by in a busy world. Even now, watching them, he saw, even felt, their boredom as they looked at their watches, as they sat playing cards, their silent wives leaving unsaid their impatience with the heat and being in such close quarters with their offspring for so long. The worst of it to Abe was his grandchildren. Instead of fishing, they were engrossed in their computer games, their eyes, without luster or wonder, glued to black boxes, their ears to discs that played strange music.

At least the youngest, Zach, was fishing, his father standing by to rebait his hook periodically. Abe watched throughout the afternoon as the boy sat cross-legged at his feet, waiting for a bite that seemed to never come. He wondered if Zach had memories of him before he became ill. Did he recall the times Abe took him in his arms and threw him in the air, catching him on the way down with hugs and kisses? Or the times they shared the same strawberry ice cream cone that Abe made, three scoops high? Zach was only a toddler when Abe sang him songs, show-tunes from the theater that the little boy seemed to love. Abe never forgot the words, "I love you Grand-Poppa," the child often murmured, clutching his blanket as he fell asleep, dreaming in the older man's arms.

Abe had dreams as well. He wanted his grandchildren to experience firsthand the waters of Eagle Lake. He wanted them to know how it felt to cast a line on still waters at sunrise when the world was first stirring and the only movements were the rustling of pheasants scampering along the shore. Would they ever know the peaceful end of a summer day, trolling back to shore...the time right before the mosquitoes forayed from their bases along the dark green algae beds, he wondered. Or when the skies at dusk formed into black menacing clouds that sparked with jolts of electric lightening. Not the kind that brought rain, but that lingered in the distance, rumbling into the night hours.

It was a new generation, Abe knew. He doubted they would feel jubilant over electric skies with electric games to keep them occupied, baseball without bats, basketball without nets. Electronically, they could be anything: conquerors, kings, at the touch of a switch.

The sun felt warm on Abe's skin. He tilted his face upwards to catch the rays and feel the spray of the water coming off the lake. He felt himself dozing. In his dream he had risen from his chair on his own power feeling strong. He marched to the middle of the boat to his chair and climbed up checking out the nooks and crannies of the bay around him. Only when he was satisfied, did he cut the motor.

He saw it was a good day for fishing. He could even see them jumping in the water, so many it looked like the surface was bubbling. Why use a reel when he could just lean over and scoop them up with net, he wondered. Too easy, he thought. He wanted a hearty fight.

Abe grabbed the reel and cast far out from the boat. Then, he waited. Seconds later the line jumped, the silver flashing under the water's surface and the line zig-zagging back and forth. Abe tugged sharply, trying to snare it, playing its maneuvers, tugging and pulling at his elusive catch. It was a big one, he thought, much heavier than he first thought and he felt himself being pulled overboard.

He snarled at the fish, taunting it, advising it to give up, shouting to all who could hear that he was Abraham, the greatest fisherman in the state of Minnesota. As if the fish comprehended, it relented, letting Abe bring him in with his line, fast, furious until it was scooped up in a net and landed with a thud on the deck. It was the biggest largemouth bass Abe had ever seen. He held it up far above his head for all to see.

Then, through his dissolving dream, he heard clapping, faint at first, but getting louder, followed by whistles and shouts. Abe felt betrayed by sleep, knowing he would awaken strapped to his chair to dead silence. But still he heard the applause as he squinted his eyes open tentatively.

Confused, he turned towards shore and caught his breath. Lined up along the shoreline, he saw the good folks of Eagle Lake waving their hats back and forth, whistling and cheering. Abe looked down at his hands, limp in his lap, bewildered, until he saw little Zach leaning against the railing standing on his toes.

Zach held up his fish, proudly displaying his catch for all to see. A baby Perch dangled from the end of the line, goldfish-sized. In one hand he waved the line, in the other he waved his white baseball cap, greeting each person as the boat drifted close to shore.

As they neared the shore the acknowledgment increased. They waved and saluted, holding up their own modest catches to the small lad on the decks of the Blue Pontoon boat. Abe watched as Zach turned to his father. Mitch applauded and hugged him, a glint in his eyes as if looking faraway. Then Zach's Uncle Thomas and the rest followed.

Mitch hugged his son again, then knelt down to meet his eyes. "The fish is too little. Send him back to his momma," he said as if repeating a magic incantation.

Zach dutifully tossed the perch back into the water. But Abe caught the boy's expression...his eyes wide, his face red with exhilaration. It was, as Abe saw and hoped, a continuation of tradition, however simple and fleeting.

On the way home, Zach crawled over to the chair next to Abe. His tiny hand found his grandfather's and overlapped it protectively. With his other hand Zach swatted gnats away from Abe's face.

Soon all the grandchildren settled in at Abe's feet. A quietness had settled over the lake, only the pontoon's motor hummed as it crossed the bay. Abe looked at his boys and their wives and children who seemed mesmerized... watching the sky of black clouds that were gathering in the distance. Rumbling, churning clouds erupted into flashes of electric light.

It had been a perfect day on Eagle Lake. Abe felt alive, surrounded by his family and reminders of the past.

The Champion

Kris Martin sat outside the Starlight Café in Whaler's Cove dreaming of the lazy days ahead—filled with sun, sand and simple pleasures. It was summer, her Kindergarten class out, and she was spending the summer at this beautiful stretch of land along the North Carolina coast with its beaches and ocean breezes. Time and the perils of weather had etched character into this coastal village, and boats of every size and shape, docked haphazardly in rows adjacent to the pier, added color. Local fisherman pulled in their catches of striped bass, bluefish and trout. Along the dunes freckle-faced-children built sand castles in the afternoon sun.

Kris spent the morning dawdling along the shop area, looking for items to fill her small cottage, a quaint lavender-painted dwelling that was all hers for the summer months. Deciding to take a break, she stopped in the village to enjoy a tall cappuccino. She dressed simply on this, her first day of vacation—black jeans and a white shirt. Even so, she could not resist wearing her turquoise rings. Their blues, the color of her own eyes, contrasted exquisitely to her almost white blonde hair which tumbled halfway down her back. Kris was in her late twenties but looked more like a teenager. Though sensitive to this, she knew the children she taught delighted in her youthful appearance, her humor and her energy.

Fifty yards away, Benny noticed her from the deck of his boat that was docked in the harbor. Sitting high in his sturdy wooden captain's chair, he studied her. A dreamy sort of girl, he thought, but the kind he knew he would never have the chance to meet. Thirty-year-old Ben Brody was the shyest man in the universe. It was a curse, he figured. Ever since he could remember he had a difficult time speaking to girls. He blushed when they looked at him. He stammered. As he grew older, he wished that he could be flippant, and speak directly into the eyes of a woman with ease. Somewhere along the way, early in life, Benny had lost his confidence. He turned inward, became quiet, a loner of sorts. "Accept the way you are, buddy" he often told himself. "You needn't stand out to make yourself known in the world." But whom was he kidding? He knew what he was. A meek, nondescript chump. And he hated it.

Benny looked at his absently moving hands on his artist pad. To his delight he found a pretty decent sketch of the pretty girl. When he looked back up and across to the girl, he saw her looking back at him. His pen froze in his hand. Before looking away, her smile found him—a quirky playful grin—then she nodded and the whole action caught him off-guard. As he turned away, he could not escape the radiated warmth of her smile. His heart melted.

Benny was mesmerized by life at the ocean's edge, its surrealism—dolphins frolicking in the surf, white dunes and picturesque lighthouses stretching for miles. The beauty of the port at Whaler's Cove had snared him while vacationing one summer, and its stories of shipwrecks and pirate lore reeled him in. He had been hooked ever since. He surveyed the inhabitants that lived in and around the boats at the harbor and liked what he saw. No suits. No ties. Just down-to-earth people with hearty laughs and sunburnt faces. The feel of the cove and the scenery was so alluring, that with every cent he had saved, Benny purchased a boat. He called it home ever since and never once looked back.

Benny was a cartoonist by trade, one of the best. He wrote stories and drew pictures for "Champions," a popular comic book that was read by children and adults across the nation. He enjoyed his work. It allowed him the freedom to create stories to his heart's content. His days were lost in imagination, writing vivid action stories that popped into his head. Sketches would follow, then the addition of vibrant colors would fill out his intriguing tales with life.

Benny was content in his work but lonely. Oh, a few friends came and went, but he longed for a true romance and often wished he could be like the characters in the stories who never seemed lacking. Maybe his standards were high, he thought. But he couldn't help dreaming only of a breathtaking woman—one to rival his most carefully drawn storybook princess—who would one day fall in love with him, and would love and appreciate his kind and gentle heart.

His dreams of passion came through in his work. Page after page of his creations were filled with scenes of valor, but of yearning as well. He would bring his super heroes into fierce battle, his words and actions for them meshing true, his larger-then-life visions springing to life with the swift brush of his sure determined hand. But his heroes were human too, like him, yearning.

At night, when the harbor was quiet and calm, when the boats sat side by side in their slips anchored under a cool coastal mist, Benny worked. He sat in his cabin under a yellow light, lulled contentedly by the boat's gentle rocking, and drew his heroic stories, his ears straining to hear the bittersweet tone of an occasional chime clinking in the night breeze and the lonely wail of a fog horn across the water.

Benny wondered what his readers would think if they knew he created his super heroes in his own wished-for mold. Though he placed them in strange and faraway lands, Benny knew he himself lived as an alien. And as he worked on his stories, his heroes and he would become one. Their unrelenting strength would be his, their fights with earth's enemies his, their praise for saving the inhabitants of the world, his.

And he was not limited by eras: in the early 1700s Benny battled the boldest, most notorious pirate, Blackbeard, who victimized ships from the Caribbean to New England. With a notorious beard that covered most of his face, Blackbeard struck terror into the hearts of his victims. The sight of him was enough to make his victims give up peacefully, turning over their ships carrying gold, silk and spices. Those who laid eyes upon the ruthless pirate cowered in fear.

But not Ben Brody. Or rather, Sir Alex, who, armed with pistols and daggers, fought all the pirate captains including Blackbeard himself. His brave fearless form almost jumped off Ben's pages. Sir Alex was not intimidated by Blackbeard's ship with its ominous skulls and crossbones. Not even the hourglass on the flag that the rogue pirate flew announcing that time was running out, its message taunting, "Death will come soon to those who cross my path."

In Benny's stories he was relentless and brave with a voice that didn't break, but was deep and commanding. He had unwavering eyes that bore deep into the souls of his adversaries. And he was respected. A man of virtue and valor.

"Hi, I'm Kris," she said standing before him on the dock.

"Ben Brody," he croaked, startled by her sudden presence at the boat.

"I noticed you drawing and I was curious," she stood taller to peek at his sketch.

Ben mumbled in low tones, gruffly, and avoided her eyes. When she didn't leave, he looked up into her eyes. In their clear blueness he could almost see his own handsome face, etched with lines and weathered from the sun, mirrored in her light-hearted direct gaze. He pulled a hand through his wild mane of wavy brown hair and tried to tuck it into his visor cap, which fell about his shoulders when he took it off to greet her.

She laughed, then waited for him to speak. An awkward silence lingered. A smile fought through his features when he decided she hadn't laughed at him.

A sideways glance. Then, "Would you—like to come on board?"

She seemed to hesitate, as if a mother's warning briefly furrowed her face, which disappeared as she hopped onto the deck of the boat. She peeked inside the galley window to the cabin below. Benny joined her and they both gazed to the tiny Christmas lights strung across the walls, blinking, though June. But she was curious and followed Benny down the steps into the cabin.

He watched her eyes widen at the sight of the rainbow of colors shouting out from the walls, the furniture, the floor. A strange, happy potpourri of colors: blues and oranges alongside reds and purples, and pink with yellow and lime-green. Her eyes scampered from his walls to his work area with its pages of drawings and the bottles of black and purple ink and sheets of paper filled the tiny cabin space.

"You're an artist," she said, breathless.

He nodded as he watched her gaze travel to the side to a row of patchwork pillows thrown over an ink-stained yellow sofa and the oddly multi-colored shag carpet laying colorful squares over a warped and weather-beaten wood floor.

"Something nice everywhere," she said, "to capture and please the eye. You wouldn't know from outside."

He smiled. "Just an old boat docked in line with a hundred others." "No, it's more. Cozy. Comfortable," she purred. "Please show me some of your work, er, a..."

"Benny," he stammered.

"I'm Kris," she said once more and reached to his side to touch his hand.

For the next half hour Benny proudly showed her his work. He exulted in her studying his creations with interest and looking through new stories that he was working on.

Suddenly, Benny noticed an odd look on her face, abrupt, surprised. She laughed

"What?" he asked.

"I've stepped into a page of one of your comic books for a minute," she replied blushing.

"You mean you think I really do live in a cluttered world of make-believe?" He blushed as well.

She took his hand. "Not like how it sounds, Benny. That I did means you have real talent...I'm impressed. You draw heroes and villains and beautiful ladies in distress. Your ship captains battle fierce storms and your dragon slayers' swords bring down giant beasts."

"Thank you, Kris," Benny said, his eyes lowering, his face even redder.

Back on deck Kris shook his hand goodbye. "It was nice meeting you. Thanks for having me on board. You are talented, Benny. Your work is the best." "Thanks again," he answered.

He was sorry see her leave so soon, but happy to have spent the short time with her. She was not only pretty, but sweet and kind as well.

"I....was....wondering...he stammered, "I was wondering if you would like to meet for coffee some time."

For a half minute she did not answer and he wondered what excuse was racing through her mind—a boyfriend, she didn't live here.

She broke the silence, "Sure." She shoved a piece of paper with her phone number into his hand. And when he looked up, she was gone.

One week passed before he had the courage to call. When he rattled off a number of coffee shops, she told him she'd rather come back aboard his boat. "If you don't mind," she added, her tone suggesting that of all the restaurants and coffee shops along the coast, she wanted to spend time in Benny's crowded cabin, with him.

"I'm honored" was all that he managed to say.

They sat side-by-side on a Sunday afternoon, on the ink-stained yellow sofa with turquoise pillows, watching old movies. She told him about her work and the children she taught in her classroom. Benny made them lunch, a favorite of the locals, tuna boats with fried okra and peanut butter milkshakes. They ate. "Delicious. A talented chef as well," she kidded.

When it was time for Kris to leave, she gave Benny a hug. "I hope you call again. I really had fun."

As the summer months passed, Benny and Kris became close. Benny was at ease in her presence. He realized that although Kris was beautiful, it was her heart that shone true and real. And he envied her children for their being able to bask in her wit and charm for the whole school year, for spending their days under her captivating spell.

The two liked to spend lazy afternoons in the village, strolling across cobblestones and browsing gift shops, buying chocolate figurines and sampling exotic flavors of ice cream. And frequenting the out of the way outside cafés. One day over coffee Kris told Benny about her family. Benny learned about Kris' overbearing mother and how Kris couldn't wait to spend this time away, by herself at the Cove. She chatted about her younger brother and cousins, then stopped, embarrassed from her rambling. "I'm sorry. You must be bored."

"Not at all," he told her.

"I'm intrigued listening to you, of watching you, of hearing of your wishes and dreams for the future." He wanted to say. But he stopped and looked down at the table.

She took his hand from across the table and squeezed.

In that moment his heart overflowed with yearning.

The time flew quickly, but both were as oblivious to its passing as they were to the faceless carnival of people around them. Across the table they saw only each other, hardly noticing the outside blur of busy movement and color.

"What about you Ben?" she asked. "Does it ever get to you? Living here alone in your boat?"

He laughed, then motioned for her to look toward the harbor. He pointed to the circus of boats, in all their variations, their tall masts weaving and jutting skyward. Then he pointed to the comical pelicans flying in a line above, soaring, dipping in playful acrobatics under a strong wind draft, and to the baby sandpipers racing in circles on the sand, playing tag at the water's edge.

She nodded. "No need to explain," she smiled.

On some days they took the boat out of the port for an afternoon ride. Miles from shore, Kris would turn up the radio and sing along to the songs, and watch Benny with amusement. "You know the words," she would chide him, "sing." But he would always decline, his face reddening with his meekness.

Then Kris would dance, her bare feet skipping across the wood deck.

On one of these days, in late afternoon, they started back for port, tired and at peace, and lulled by the warmth of their companionship and the rays of the Atlantic sun.

Benny was angry with himself. How he wished he could muster courage enough to speak the words to let Kris know his true feelings for her. Did she share them? he wondered. For once in his life he cursed his make-believe world of myth and folklore — the world that forbade him to speak to reality.

He shook his head in frustration. And shame, and yet still savored each moment they spent together. Yes, he told himself, he and Kris were friends, but he longed to see the spark one day in her eyes that their relationship had changed its course. Until then, he knew he would wait. And hope.

It was late August. Despite the unusually brisk sea breeze, the air aboard hung heavy. Soon, Benny lamented, Kris would return inland to her teaching job and her days would be filled with classroom activities. Their days together were nearing an end.

"Let's go out of the harbor today," she suggested when he met her at mid- morning.

The morning sun had disappeared in a light drizzle. Benny looked out over the water and saw dark grey clouds hovering in the distance. "You think it's a good idea?" he asked, trying to ignore how badly he wanted to be with her on the water. "We don't have to go out too far. This may be our last voyage for a while," she said.

Benny fired up the engines, and, dressed in hooded sweatshirts, they headed out to sea.

A few miles out the clouds parted and the sun shone through above them. Hoping for a clear afternoon, he kept heading out farther. Kris meanwhile had turned up the radio and sang until her voice became tired and raspy.

Towards late afternoon dark clouds began gathering. The boat started rocking over heavy swells. They realized they were out too far and started to head back, but the distant storm that was now gathering strength, pounded down on them. Rain and wind lashed out. Benny's small craft was no match for the gusts and the force of the pelting rain. Down below in the cabin, he heard bottles of his precious ink slide off the shelves and crash to the floor with each sideways pitch. As they did, he couldn't help thinking his fantasy world was slipping away as if his last weapons were being destroyed

He looked at Kris who was holding her stomach and grimacing in pain. The tiny damp quarters suddenly became claustrophobic. Benny watched Kris poke her head out of the porthole for air while he fought with the wheel trying to steer them away from the battering fifty-foot waves.

"We can't turn around, what do we do?" Kris screamed when she pulled her water-soaked head back in apparently realizing the true danger for the first time, a helpless and scared expression on her face.

"We have to break the wave, to ride over the top!" Benny yelled, trying to steady the boat from each slamming force. Kris tried to steady herself by grabbing the wood railing. But with each pitch she was tossed, forward to aft, then side to side. He watched in horror as she slid across the deck like a rag doll.

Once, she landed against the wall with a heavy thud, hitting her head. A trickle of blood slid down her cheek from her brow. "It's not that bad," she told Benny when he momentarily took his hands from the wheel, "get us through this Captain." She managed a smile, but Benny could almost feel her pain.

"We're on our own!" Benny yelled, motioning to the radio and instrument panel which had taken a hit by snapping wires and falling beams and was now flooded and useless. The windows to the cabin were broken. Benny knew the coastguard would not be searching for them. He often took the boat out overnight and stayed docked in other ports along the coast. It was up to him to bring them back to safety.

Benny's hands were swollen and bleeding from gripping the wheel. Kris, trembling and covered by cold water and debris, tried to help. But Benny, thinking only of her, tried to open a side cupboard for a wool blanket to wrap it around her. He held her close to him with one arm, as he struggled for control of the wheel with the other. It had been four hours and the storm showed no signs of letting up.

Even as night was upon them, the rain fell steadily. They pitched and rolled in the angry sea. He tried to meet each giant wave with a sharp turn away. As each wave attacked Benny screamed out, daring it to overtake them. Kris watched in amazement, respecting the demanding tone from the man-in-charge.

Benny fought the storm as if he was in battle with Blackbeard himself. He took control and taunted the fierce and able pirate, who in the darkness, had forty guns mounted in his direction on his ship's rail. Although they were on the brink of such danger, Benny would not succumb to the terror. For Kris's life was at stake. His lady's.

Destruction surrounded them. The cabin floor was plastered with Benny's drawings. They lay in torn and crumpled heaps, colors bled together across soaked pages. His heroes in action were lost under layers of sea water. Unrecognizable, they were only cloudy smudges as ink and water became one.

Hour after hour they fought the black walls of the sea. Then, at last, after battling through the night, the wind gales began to lessen. The waves lost their menacing force. The sheets of cold rain turned to steady drops, then a gentle mist. Dawn was breaking and the Carolina coastline appeared after being hidden in dense fog. Benny peered in the distance. He swore there was a tinge of smoke in the air, as if the remnants of a cannon's blast.

The sky was a strange mixture of morning hues, overshadowing the last of the ominous storm clouds. Benny sat at the helm with Kris by his side. He guided the broken vessel towards shore, careful to avoid the viselike grip of the coastal sand and ragged rocks that lay ahead.

Benny was battered from the storm's fury, but felt a renewed sense of bravery. He had found his voice. His strength. His courage. He was ready now to confess to expose his feelings that he had kept hidden for so long.

He turned to Kris, soaked with perspiration, his forehead cut with the splinters of wood from the gale. Bruised and exhausted, but a true Champion, a real-life hero. He started to speak, but Kris shook her head, quieting him. Instead, she reached for his hand and held it tight. At that moment, something beautiful passed between them. It was as if her heart opened, letting him in with all his hopes and dreams of grandeur. For in her eyes, he saw the sign that he had been searching for.

Her simple touch was everything He had slain the dragon. He had climbed the highest mountain. He brought his lost ship in to shore and at last, captured the heart of his beautiful princess.

The two headed to shore, the silence between them growing. But even without words, the silence spoke — of tenderness, of adoration, and of a new beginning.

Pillar of Strength

He was a lean, mean, evil-tempered teenager, his arms pocked with tattoos of skulls and crossbones, his face and tongue pierced with silver studs. Thick jet-black hair, long and wild, shrouded his face and shielded his dark squinting eyes and sneer. His name was Derek. He was the kind one side-stepped — avoided entirely, if possible — since he looked like trouble. He was.

Derek lived with his grandmother, Louise, with whom he shared a small two-bedroom home in St. Louis, along the west bank of the Mississippi River. Louise took the boy in as a toddler after his parents were killed in a car accident. It had been a horrible time. Though the deaths wrung her heart, she also cried for her grandson and his uncertain future, a future that lay in her hands.

He was a handful, for he came to her when he was in the "terrible twos" stage of life. But, back then, she had the strength to keep up with him.

Widowed for many years before he came, the sound of his voice and his endless abundance of energy cheered and challenged her, and filled her long and lonely days.

Louise was both mother and father to her grandson. From first grade on, she helped him with his homework. On cold winter afternoons she made him his favorite drink, hot chocolate with whipped cream. In the summer heat she sweltered in the stands with the other parents at the school ball park. She cheered Derek's base hits and fielding, and even when he struck out, she yelled words of encouragement. Win or lose, she would always take him out for strawberry ice cream on the way home.

But her favorite times with Derek were on those August summer nights when she would take him out the river's edge where they would sit on a grassy bluff in a warm gentle river breeze and look out over the waters of the Mississippi. There, under the wide-spread crown of an oak tree, they would watch in amazement as fireflies danced above them under the glare of the moon. It was a magical place, a magical time. Quiet and serene, the only sound would be the methodical river-water as it lapped upon the shore. "This could be heaven, you know," she would whisper as she cuddled her sleepy boy in her arms.

But as Derek grew older their trips to the bluff lessened. Tending to his needs was exhausting and Louise was no longer young and healthy. She had suffered for years with an irregular heartbeat and depended on her medication to get her through the day. Bouts of crippling arthritis were also now part of her daily existence. She tried bending and stretching like her doctor advised, but some days it was an effort just to get out of bed in the morning. Derek needed her, however, and she knew she would never let him down. Even on her worst days, she was there for him. Her devotion to the child knew no bounds.

As Derek grew taller into his pre-teen years Louise continued to shower him with praise and affection. But his responsiveness dwindled. When she offered him a spontaneous hug, he rebuffed her and became like an ice-statue in her arms. The more she tried to do for him, the more he pulled away. Until one day, unable to make the walk to the river alone, she asked him to take her to the serene bluff, where she knew his tension didn't stand a chance to brew at the water's edge. Instead, he grew angry and refused her outright. She never asked again. She was learning his ways.

When Derek was fourteen, he came down with pneumonia and almost lost his life. For days he lingered in the hospital, struggling for breath under a plastic tent. Louise never left his side. She slept in the next bed in his room from which she would rush in to hold his hand during the late hours when he would cry out in his delirium and fear. On those nights she would gently stroke his face and whisper in his ear, telling him that it would be alright. "Don't be afraid. Grandma's here."

To everyone's surprise, Derek rallied and made a full recovery. Louise was grateful and thanked God each night for saving her grandson.

As he grew into his later teen years, she encountered more problems. More and more sullen and moody, Derek became reclusive, spending more and more time alone in his room. He started smoking, even though he knew the second-hand smoke in the small home caused Louise to cough and wheeze. She knew he was sneaking out late at night and coming in early in the morning. At least once a week the school called letting her know that he was truant. But when she tried to talk with him about it, he became loud and abusive and pounded his fists on the walls. "Stay out of my life!" he screamed.

As he turned seventeen, his appearance worsened. Baggy, dirty clothes hung shapelessly around his lanky body and his hair grew even longer. It lay wild about his shoulders. Derek went out of his way to be mean to Louise. He often left his shoes in her pathway, causing her to trip and fall. He turned his stereo loud at night so that she would be forced to lay in bed awake for hours from the pounding noise. If she approached him and tried to talk with him about it, he became loud and obnoxious, oftentimes screaming in her face and frightening her.

"What have I done?" she would ask herself. "Where did I go wrong?"

She yearned to speak with her grandson civilly, to understand where his anger was coming from. Sometimes when he was not aware, she stole glances at him and her heart ached. For underneath the hard decorations that adorned his body, behind his menacing look and demeanor, he was a handsome young man. He favored his father, she thought, with his piercing dark brown eyes and strong chin. If only she could reach him, tell him things were okay, that the world was not his enemy, that there was love and happiness buried somewhere inside him and he needn't look far to find it. But she could not. Maybe someday he will come back to me, she prayed, hopefully soon.

One night late, past midnight, she felt a heaviness through her body. Sadness crept through her weary limbs as she closed her eyes and began to drift off to sleep. Her pillows were positioned on each side of her head to cover her ears, as they were every night, to block the pulsating sound coming from Derek's room.

The song tonight blasting through the door was by a rock group called Death Creature. Derek's favorite. He listened to their song lyrics, over and over for hours on end. Tonight, was no exception. She winced as the words crept into her brain, "Welcome creature, hear my cry...save me from this awful lie...even evil has a place...welcome creature, show your face."

Derek lay on his bed, on his back staring up at the ceiling. The window was shut tightly and the shades drawn, making his tiny room humid and almost suffocating. A black light in the corner gave the room a dingy, purple haze. Just as he liked it—his space, his music—overtaking his very being.

As Death Creature screamed their message, Derek relaxed, beads of sweat now trickling down his flushed face. He tried to remember how long ago he had taken the pink pill, but time and logic were quite out of reach. Jake had slipped him the downer when they were at the bowling alley earlier. Derek shoved it deep in his pocket to take later. "The stars will come visiting," Jake had promised.

Derek now knew that he was right.

He tried to smile, but his lips felt strange and rubbery. He felt his throat open and close in spasms involuntarily, causing him to panic. A heaviness began creeping throughout his body. Within minutes he found that he had no strength at all. He could not even lift his arms or legs. The numbness slowly made its way throughout, shutting down his muscles and nerves and before long he lay in a completely paralyzed state. He sucked in a deep breath and tried to scream for help, but out came a hushed whisper. "I'm going to die," Derek thought as his heart pounded through his chest.

Death Creature screamed at him and the pounding of their lyrics were now torture to his ears. His body lay limp and lifeless. He soon realized that Jake's pill was worse than death. It had imprisoned him in his own body, his mind the only organ left to let him know what it felt like to be buried alive. Over and over, he tried to scream, inhaling a breath, then arranging his mouth to form the word.... "Grandma!!!"

He didn't remember how long he had been trying to call for her. Derek knew it might be hours before she would look in his room. He wondered what her reaction would be, and his heart sank. It would be payback time. If she chose, she could do absolutely nothing to help him, but watch him die a slow and torturous death. He couldn't blame her. Why should she want to save him? She would be free of his evil forever, free from his taunting, morose behavior. Why would a sick old woman want to assist the very devil-child who made her daily existence a living hell?

Derek's mind began to wander. He imagined her caring for him with the same indifference that he had with her. How many times had he ignored her request for a simple glass of water? It would have been easy to bring her two aspirin on the days she lay aching in pain. And he could have sat with her, late at night on the bluff, even for a few minutes while she reveled in the joy of being with him and watching the river flow by. Now, he thought, he would be dependent on her for his every breath — she whom he emotionally tortured, she, who had every right to turn her back on him in disgust.

The pulsating rhythm from Death Creature was driving him mad. Over and over the lyrics screamed, playing off his over-sensitive brain. Then, just when he thought he might be driven completely insane, the crushing sound ceased. The room became light from the glare of the morning sun. A fresh breeze entered, cooling the stifling air.

Straining his eyes to one side, he saw her standing beside him in her tattered robe and heard her soft and gentle voice as she spoke to him, telling him that it would be alright. She stroked his cheek with her hand and moved a strand of hair that had fallen across his face. With a corner of the damp sheet, she wiped at the perspiration that gathered in pools around his neck. A tear slid from the corner of his eye when he heard the familiar words. "Don't be afraid...grandma's here."

From that moment on, Derek was moved by her unconditional devotion to his physical and emotional needs. For, although frail and weak herself, Louise catered to the demands of his condition. She mustered every ounce of strength she could to lift his limbs, pulling them, massaging and exercising them. She took him for walks in his chair in the afternoon sun and brought him tall glasses of iced tea. Louise cut Derek's food in tiny pieces so that it would be easier for him to chew. She talked to him, promising that he would one day be well, headstrong and feisty once again.

Time was all Derek had and he used it to study the angel-woman who was trying to bring him back to life. He noticed her fingers knotted from arthritis, and he wondered how long she had been suffering. She couldn't weigh more than ninety pounds, yet somehow, she managed to bathe him and lift him from his chair to his bed. Guilt plagued him, for he had all the time in the world to relive the nasty things he had done to her over the years.

He was born angry. Derek couldn't remember a time when he was truly happy or content. He felt the physical loss of his parents when he was growing up. Although he couldn't recall them emotionally, the photographs placed around the house were a constant reminder of what he had and lost. The other kids often teased him, calling him an orphan and saying nasty things about having to live with his "old granny" Louise. Instead of appreciating his grandmother, he felt sorry for himself and took his angry moods out on the one person who had loved him unconditionally for as long as he could remember.

Sobs wracked his throat when he thought of how shabbily he had treated her. What a kind, beautiful lady she was. He saw her now, for the first time, her silver hair tied back in a neatly wrapped bun. She smelled of scented soap, lilac, and her smell calmed him when she walked by. Without her he was alone, for not a friend came by to wish him well. Had it not been for his grandmother, he would have withered deeper into his scared and vulnerable mind and eventually died. "If I ever find the strength, I will make it up to her," he vowed. "I will spend my life giving her the love and respect she deserves."

The air in his room seemed warmer now and the smoky, stuffy atmosphere was overpowering. Laying flat on his back, he stared up at the ceiling and became angry because the lyrics from Death Creature were interrupting his thoughts. The music was getting louder and he was screaming for it to stop. The sound of his strong and clear voice startled him and Derek's eyes widened. He turned his head easily from side to side, then tried to move his fingers and toes. They wiggled about at his command and he let out a scream of joy.

Slowly, Derek inched his way off his bed and stood on his feet. He wavered a bit unsteadily, but his balance returned within a few seconds. His phone rang and the machine picked up a message. It was Jake, wanting to meet him later as if nothing unusual happened. Derek ran about his cluttered room and jumped up and down with joy when he realized he had been dreaming. The pill Jake had given him took him down to the scariest depths of fear and stark realization. But it was all a dream, just a horrible dream. He laughed, running in circles, then opened the window and turned off the stereo that had been playing through the night.

Louise. His thoughts immediately went to his grandmother. Derek knew now that there would be time to make things right. He ripped the dirty clothes from his body and searched through his clothes for something clean and presentable to wear. He found a pair of clean jeans and a blue shirt that buttoned down the front. Gathering his wild mane of hair, he brushed it and secured it neatly into a ponytail. She would be shocked by his appearance, but it was where he wanted to start.

This morning, Derek would make her breakfast, her favorite, cinnamon toast and apple tea. After kissing her good morning, he would sit down with her and apologize for his behavior and ask for her forgiveness.

Derek threw open the door and ran about the house looking for Louise. It was strangely quiet. Usually at this hour she was up, sitting at the table and reading the morning paper. He checked the backyard, then the front, but she was nowhere to be found. He called her name. No answer. As he checked her room once again, he thought he saw her robe laying on the floor next to her bed. But Derek's breath caught in his throat when he approached it, for it was Louise herself laying in her robe, slumped in a lifeless heap on the floor. Her body was limp and heavy. Only her eyes moved. They told of the terror she was experiencing, trapped in a prison of bones and flesh.

She lay exactly where she had fallen, curled in a fetal position. Derek fumbled with the phone and called for help. "Please hurry!" he yelled. Derek knelt before his grandmother and cradled her head in his lap. Her grey eyes widened like saucers, seeming to search his face for answers. He felt her tremble like a frightened animal as she struggled to speak without results. Her mouth formed a circle, but no audible sound escaped.

Derek tried to comfort her, speaking to her softly. He told her that he would stay with her, that help was on the way. Then he turned so she could not see his tears or hear the muffled sob that escaped his lips. How could he live if she left him now? There was so much he wanted to do for her, so much more he wanted to say. He held her tight and whispered words that he knew she would understand. "Don't be afraid, Derek's here."

The trees along the river front were already starting to change. The blue-green leaves of the giant oak had a purple tinge and the branches were starting to droop at an angle towards the ground. Two lone figures sat on the bluff overlooking the Mississippi. It was dark and still...but for the rhythmic lapping of the water as it hit the shore. There was no heartache. No pain. Only joy and love. Was it heaven? It was just as she pictured it. The grass beneath was plush, soft as velvet. A gentle wind blew. And the fireflies danced, under the glare of the Missouri moon.

Trappings

Seashells lay scattered along the south Florida shore. Michael sauntered barefoot on the sand, eyes cast down, closely scrutinizing those he wanted to take with him, a memory of beauty. He chose soft coral ones, some with smooth surfaces in colors of pinks and browns. He added a few Sand Dollars and a small starfish to his growing collection, dropping them into a deep suede pouch. He and these shells had shared the same waters—rested on the same stretch of land. When he took them out again, he and his family would be thousands of miles from this longtime home. But he would display his collection out in the open; they were his link to his incredible times. The seashells, he hoped, would comfort, and get him through the days of uncertainty that lay ahead.

The Hayes had it all—wealth, power, and the trappings that went with it. As beautiful people they rubbed elbows for years with the rich and famous. They lived in a perfect world, a world of big money, palatial estates and fast imported cars. When they were not traveling, for business or pleasure, Michael and Colette Hayes were the favorites of the Tropics, a wealthy community playground set up against the Atlantic shore. The couple, in their mid-thirties, did not look like the parents of their school-age twin boys, Cooper and Cameron. Rather, Michael looked as if he had just stepped off a Hollywood set with his deep black hair and eyes, and year-round tan. His tan, his private vanity, provided the backdrop for his signature-look gold chains that would lay comfortably on his exposed chest. Though full Irish, he emanated the Mediterranean, his deep black eyes hypnotic. Colette would often call him Omar Sharif in intimate moments, giggling. Always dressed immaculately in cashmere sweaters, designer jeans and snake-skin shoes, he carried himself like the success he was. Yet his most cherished prize was not the gold watches or four carat diamond rings that he sported, but his stunning wife, Colette. She turned heads with her beauty, and kept them turned with her elusive style, reminiscent of a young Jackie Kennedy. Brown hair streaked with blends of golds and browns, she exuded confidence and magnetism—a woman, a lady, comfortable in her own skin. She moved with certainty and charm whether in a simple shirt, pants and sandals, or in a black silk evening gown with delicate rhinestone slippers.

Butlers greeted their visitors. Maids, housekeepers and gardeners kept in the background of the Hayes palace, but each did his or her duty to make sure every room that looked out to spectacular seascape views, all, was as impeccable as the Hayes were themselves. The couple owned a yacht and were members of the most exclusive country clubs.

But all that was gone now. A failed business venture had stripped them of most everything, taking them from riches to rags in just six short months—a fast and frightening roller-coaster fall into a nightmare of Middle America, far from the Tropics. Now, just having arrived, the Hayes were strangers in a strange land: a run-down city halfway between the two coasts. Colette sat on the floor of a bleak apartment, sorting through their belongings, watching Michael's fingers trail without life through his seashell collection, his eyes blank.

Colette recalled the night this fall seemed imminent, when it was finally obvious to her something was terribly wrong. She had primed her ears to Michael's not often hushed tones as his voice rose and fell inside his office suite before hearing the phone slam against the cradle. Frozen, she listened to him pick it up minutes later, and to the subsequent next strained conversation. Curious, she left their bed and crept down the hallway, her slippers noiseless on the thick padded carpet. She stood quietly outside his office door and listened, and heard the fragments of his desperate conversation. She realized he was trying desperately to patch together the remaining pieces of his business, and wasn't doing a good job at it. He was out of control, she knew, a possibility so new to her. In his magnificent office suite he floundered alone, without her, his hushed tones betraying his wish she should be spared.

"Not my home," she heard his voice crack in a lame threat, then plea. His next words were muffled, until the words, "layoffs, restructuring, creditors." Then came her husband's biting off his short sentences with tears.

Soon, she knew, would come big and irreversible changes, changes neither she nor her husband would have control over. And their home was the cornerstone of this disaster — Michael's dream home, the thirty-room mansion on seven acres, replete with movie theater, tennis courts, Olympic pool and customized billiard room, all surrounded by beautiful terraced gardens. Something from a movie set, she thought looking around in the dim hall, but quite real, theirs. Michael had purchased it for fifteen million dollars. "A drop in the bucket," he had teased, the pride in his voice unmistakable for he had earned every dollar he put down for the down payment from his thriving corporation, Hayes Enterprises.

"Thank our lucky stars," he would tell her when they stood on their balcony on warm summer nights, dressed in matching silk robes and sipping champagne. And they would toast the sky. "To our good fortune, and the future..."

"And the boys," she would add with a twinkle.

And their toasts and future hopes and dreams would drift amidst the soothing ocean breezes and scents of jasmine.

But as Colette would dutifully thank their lucky stars, she would murmur a silent prayer. For although her cherished Michael swathed her in rich trappings, it was not what meant the most to her. No, it was the intimate times they shared, the times they sat talking close together on the couch in front of the fire, or had coffee and read the Times together on a Sunday morning. The working day was far away, then his funny expressions unguarded, amusing, his Omar Sharif facade dissolving in his childlike animation as he would roll his eyes in mock despair as he spoke.

That their extravagant lifestyle seemed temporary forever lingered in the back of her mind. No matter. She appreciated the grandness around her, but took it in stride. She focused on the real things: tending to Michael when he became ill, to buying costumes for the boys at Halloween. In Colette's heart, a home was not about outer acreage, but about the passion radiating from within the walls. She had always tried to relay her feelings to Michael. But more and more he became driven, immersing himself in the continuing desire to succeed.

And now, tonight, she knew they would be put to the test. Because Colette realized that Hayes Enterprises was spiraling into a crisis.

Hayes Enterprises was a thriving investment company that catered to millionaires, successful in making the rich richer. Her husband built it from a crazy fledgling brainstormed concern in college, into a billion-dollar company. He designed a trading post of financial research, hiring teams of young people movers and shakers whose ideas helped him make fortunes for others and themselves. The company became wealthy with speed and ease, their dividends exploding to enormous heights in a short time, creating an atmosphere of euphoria. Each month Hayes Enterprises created more and wealth for their investors worldwide.

Then, they were hit with skyrocketing production costs. Competing firms after unlocking Hayes' keys to their wild success, then mimicked, undercut, and stole major clients by any means necessary, something Colette knew Michael avoided. Instead, he tried to scale back Hayes, then reorganized, but was struggling. Their stock began to collapse and when news of their battles hit the media, loans were called in.

Michael was forced to borrow more money to pay them back. He was caught in a vicious circle, borrowing from friends and strangers. Each large sum of money loaned to him was put back into the business. It was never enough since there was little profit to work off the loans, and no more clear working capital. The loans he borrowed from others started the fall. It soon had a domino effect and within months, others started to lose their homes as well.

Michael tried to protect Colette at first, shielding her from the threatening phone calls. "We'll be okay," he would tell her gently in subsequent days when she walked in on him during a bad call. "I'll find a way out of this."

A week later the truck arrived at their estate. Debtors took it all, furniture, rugs, art objects and paintings from the walls. Then Michael confessed, they had lost their home. Creditors were lining up against him. It would take him the rest of two lives to pay everyone back. But he was a moral man. He swore that he would, even if it were five dollars a week. Only then could he live with himself.

Colette stared at the stacked cardboard boxes that littered the rooms of their tiny apartment, an obstacle course of stuffed clothes, dishes and children's toys. She pulled her jacket around her in the damp room as the small heater cranked on once again. It was October and an autumn chill swept the area, bringing with it dreary skies and light drizzle. She would have relished gusts of cold air blowing in through the window. Even a simple draft would do. It seemed impossible, for their only outside view was the flat brick wall of the next building.

She sat on the brown stained carpet against one end of the room trying to see Michael at the other end whose face was now turned away from her. She knew the face that would be staring back at hers, his lips trying to force a smile. His eyes, once clear and perceptive now stared absent. She knew without looking that his head would shake back and forth every so often in disbelief and that his shoulders would sag. He carried the worries of the world upon them.

Colette wanted to push the boxes aside and march over to him. She wanted to sit next to him on the floor and take him in her arms. She wanted to assure him, to tell him it was not the end of the world, that they still had each other and the boys. She wanted to comfort. They were still a family. But she had said it before and the words seemed to hover in front of him, not sinking in. He seemed to hear her and appreciate her gestures, but he remained even now stunned by their turn of events and emotionally guarded, as if he could not trust his emotions. He would thank her politely for telling him that other great businesses were lost in the blink of an eye, and yes, he knew there were ways to begin again. She wanted to let him know it was not the perpetual party they came from that meant so much to her. It was Michael the husband and father.

She knew how much he loved her, how he treated her like a princess when they were dating and a queen after they were married. He even provided the castle for her to live in. "Are you happy?" he asked her time and again. "Yes, Michael, I'm happy." And they would kiss.

More important to Colette was that Michael was a loving father, how he chummed with his children, clowned, embraced them with warmth often, even if his face carried the blankness that seemed perpetual these days.

Now, Michael needed her. He had always been the strong one, the decision maker. But his fortress was crumbled and she was fighting daily to break through the new wall he was building around himself. She wondered if this were possible.

What would it take, Colette wondered? How could she get through to him? She wanted to shake him in frustration. "I don't need rubies. I don't need diamonds. I need you," she had said often and futilely. He didn't believe her...she could see it in his eyes. "I've failed you." She shuddered thinking of the future, with Michael locked in this fog. How could he relate to the boys? They needed him too.

Colette surveyed the two-bedroom apartment rented to them as a favor by Michael's brother, Alex. "Just until you get on your feet again," Alex told his brother. She knew Michael hated asking his kid brother for help, but he would be abroad with buddies for a year and his apartment would be vacant. It was theirs, no questions asked.

Michael agreed to the move. He wanted Colette and the boys far away from Florida where he was besieged by angry accusations —many from those he once considered friends. The Hayes' names had been stripped from the memberships at the country clubs, taken off plaques and rosters, but still spoken of, in gossip—in rumors and scandal at parties to which they were no longer invited.

She wondered what any of the backbiters would say if and when they learned where the Hayes had landed, in a building stretched across a street of cracked sidewalks, lined with blinking neon signs and billboards. She looked across the room to the grimy window, hearing the clamoring outside. It was a noisy neighborhood, replete with hot dog stands, corner markets and deli's. Cars sounded on the streets below, the neighbors, above and below and through the walls. It was a dissonance of residents, cars, alley cats and "hectic life." Inside were walls of chipped paint and a tiny square of kitchen floor slapped together with misshapen tiles. Light bulbs without fixtures swung above them from the water-stained ceiling bathing the rooms a dim yellow haze.

Her thoughts dissolved when she stared back at her task at hand—the boxes marked in black ink with ladling lists scrawled across the cardboard. It was strange seeing her belongings lumped together, squashed in a square space and tossed about on a truck, only to be plunked down in front of her in new surroundings. She noticed her name scrawled across one. The box was open, clothes spilling out on the floor. She looked at her clothes, silks and satins, and designer shoes with jewels. It was all so inconsequential now. She felt like Dorothy from the Wizard of Oz, caught up in a spinning cyclone, traveling through space and being dropped down to another time and place.

Colette was thankful that the boys were oblivious. Immediately upon arrival they began chasing each other through the cramped quarters, playing tag among the disarray. Colette tried to hush them, thinking their squeals and shouts would grate on Michael's nerves, worrying that their commotion would intensify his dismal mood. But he didn't even seem to notice their happy chaos.

His face turned back now she saw him gazing at a collection of shells that he had brought with him. It was these shells he unpacked first and had been dawdling with for the past two hours, arranging them on a small table in the corner. It was if he was arranging a shrine, she thought with some alarm. Seashells of every size and shape were positioned just so. As she watched Michael would pick one up, examine it, measure it in his hand.

Michael touched the few grains of sand that fell from the seashells. He gathered them in his cupped hand and gently poured it back into the crevices. He imagined them scattered along the shore beneath his estate. The warm summer tide playing... pulling them back and bringing in new ones with each wave. Holding one close to his ear Michael tried to hear the echo of the sea, but it was silent.

Someone knocked on the door, startling Colette from her observation of her husband. "Come in" she yelled, her exhaustion preventing her from going to the door.

The door creaked open and a child stood in the doorway. His face was dirty and he wiped his runny nose with the end of his shirt sleeve. A large bulldog sat at his side. "Winston," he told them, introducing his pet, then smiled, displaying a set of missing front teeth.

"Would you like to come in?" Colette asked.

The tiny child did and gawked about, sizing up the room, the boxes, the children who had stopped their roughhousing and Michael sitting sullen over his collection on the floor. When he saw Michael, the boy hesitated until three more kids rushed in behind him. One, a larger child about her boy's age, carried a carved pumpkin that he held out to Cameron. "I'm Spike."

"Hi. I'm Cameron." Cameron smiled, then laughed.

"Cooper."

The introductions quick, all the boys entered, the dog Winston followed. Colette smiled and warmed at the sight of the now laughing kids and the sounds of thundering sneakers running through the maze.

"And I'm Missus Kramer, your upstairs neighbor."

Colette turned back to the door where a plump woman with grey hair and kind eyes stood juggling a lumpy plate. " I made you an apple pie."

Colette jumped up and ushered the lady in, thanking her.

"Jack Stafford," a gravelly voice rumbled from the hallway, making his way inside. "Maintenance. Welcome." He chewed on a soggy cigar that never left his mouth as he spoke.

Suddenly the room was smaller, cozier, alive.

Mrs. Kramer was admiring Colette's clothes that were strewn about the boxes. "These are just adorable," she exclaimed, examining the suede jackets and jeweled shoes. Mr. Stafford began examining the walls and ceilings for repair. The giggling boys and a drooling Winston played hide and seek among the boxes.

If Michael were to come apart it would be now, Colette thought. Right at this moment when the entire universe crashed in on the tiny hopeless planet he must live in. He couldn't run. He couldn't hide. There was not one spot left in their quarters to retreat.

"Dad, where can we put our pumpkin?" Cooper asked. He held the heavy pumpkin with a crooked carved grin in his sagging arms. Everyone began looking for a space- a counter top, a patch on the floor, but all was taken. Faces gravitated to the table where the seashells lay, waiting it seemed for the obvious — for Michael to scoop up the trinkets.

"Dad!" Cameron urged. Michael hesitated.

What was he clinging to? He asked himself. Perhaps the memory of the ocean he lived near and loved while his life was at lowest ebb. But why hold on to shells when he had real pearls at his side? Invaluable ones, treasures loved and protected by a softer shell that with his help, would solidify over time. In one sweep he gathered them in his hands. Michael noticed the neighbor boys looking at them. "Here," he offered. "Trick or Treat." They grabbed them from his hands, examining them-trading with each other, then stuffed them deep inside their pockets.

The room became a noisy spectacle of activity and commotion. Young and old voices spoke simultaneously opposing and in harmony, ebbing and flowing–squeals, bartering, jeers. Life danced in their new home. Over it all

Winston's yelps and howls harmonized the melee, made sense of it.

Colette approached her Michael spurred by a spark in his eyes she noticed across the room. She faced him. No mistake, she thought, that spark blazed anew from his Omar Sharif eyes, an unguarded Omar.

He was back, she knew. A sweet surrender.

"Are you happy?" she asked him, then laughed, waiting for a break in the stoic mask. Did he see the new adventure of days, the new enterprise, a new enterprise without baubles and beads, and gold chains, but one based on inner strength? It wouldn't be easy. But she knew together they could make it happen- that they could once again feel peace at the end of the day.

"Happy?" he repeated the word.

He didn't answer and she didn't expect him to. It was an inconceivable question. She watched him glance around the room, smile, and roll his eyes. Then he did what other men had done in times as ancient as the oceans.

He took his wife in his arms and he kissed her.

Alien Heart

The planet Daxon was a celestial body located halfway between Jupiter and Mars. Icy and barren, a hardy race of intelligent creatures had somehow evolved over time. How the Daxonians came about no one knew, but they persevered and multiplied. Though only four thousand in number, they were a powerful group, with the stamina to survive their barely habitable conditions.

Their physical characteristics favored survival. Daxonians were tall, physically strong, and ruthless. Their exteriors, a tough, thick and leathery skin, extended all the way down to the fingers and toes of their arm and leg extensions. Each Daxonian had a circular eye on the front part of an oval head that never stopped moving. The eye moved about in a rapid nervous manner, constantly on the lookout for danger. A Daxonian eye could spot an enemy approaching within a split second, from any direction.

Their blood-sworn enemies were the Glitans, who were as tough as the Daxonians. They were giant ant-like creatures with bodies as hard as diamonds. The Glitans would relish their ambushes during which they would hide behind dunes or deep within caves, then appear without warning to slaughter the Daxonians. They killed as much for sport as for necessity. The payoff was brutal: within seconds of attack, their Daxonian prey would be crushed to mere puddles of unrecognizable sludge. Yet, with their superior reflexes and sharpened skills for survival, the Daxonians lived. But it was a deplorable existence.

And now time was running out. The source of the two species' enmity was water. What little water remained on the planet was congregated along the outer lowland areas. It was hoarded and fought over, but the Daxonians knew it was only a matter of time till it would be depleted. So, when word came of a flourishing planet called Earth...with a vast amount of water, they knew it was time to investigate.

Two expeditions crossed the universe to study Earth from above, and the Earth-beings. But both times the Earthlings spotted the Daxonians, who then quickly aborted their respective missions without the needed data. Soon after, the leaders held a meeting to devise a solution. Their ruling member, Roan of the Highest Order, outlined a foolproof plan: a small crew would leave on their mother ship for Earth. Once there, one of their kind would be left to live among these curious creatures, disguised in humanistic form. In this strange form, their spy would be free to collect scientific and cultural data and in time bring it back to Daxon. And this information would ensure the survival for which they were so hungry. Roan added that the mission would take 365 earth-days.

One of their best was chosen for the mission, Leel, known for her strength and courage. Because of this, and her intelligence and training, she would be outfitted as an "Earth Woman." In order to pass as an Earth woman, their scientists would adorn her in the soft-human-like covering they called "skin," a head shield called "hair," and not one, but two working eyes. Soon she was ready to make the voyage to the distant land.

Leel's mate, Tark, watched with curiosity as she stood before him ready to enter the ship for the journey across the universe.

She stopped once and turned to look at him. He nodded to her his acknowledgment. She held the gaze and she knew he wished her well. Their connection at that moment was powerful. It meant, "Be careful-be strong-be well." It was fast and fleeting, for expressions of emotions among their kind were discouraged and reserved only for the pains of survival and war.

Still, Leel was aware and was grateful Tark's nod meant more than was allowed on Daxon. By it Leel knew how much he feared for her safety and would feel the loss during her time on the distant journey. She knew and was glad Tark was the one designated to meet her on the planet's surface at the end of her mission, glad, even though his life would be at risk there, and there were no guarantees.

The door of the ship had hardly slammed shut when the process of transforming Leel into a female human form began. She was raised high above the ship on a platform for all to see. When it was completed, she reeled in uncertainty when she saw and heard those below gasp in horror at the curved female form that stood above them with the two eyes that moved in unison. A signal came from Roan of the Highest Order and the platform was lowered at once.

It was the first year of the 21st Century. Summer had arrived in the rural city of Jewell, England—a place of timeless tranquility, spread along the River Willow. Quaint surroundings encompassed ancient farmsteads and sleepy hamlets. The streets overflowed with bursts of colorful flowers, and picturesque churches hid themselves in ivy among the slopes and valleys. Today the sky was a deep blue, adorned with smatterings of cottony white clouds.

People moved about, chattering among themselves. It was a delightful afternoon and children and adults were out and about the main street through town. The favorite meeting place was a fruit and vegetable market where vendors proudly displayed their goods. Tourists and townspeople alike poked and prodded the produce, stopping to taste samples of purple plums and ripe strawberries. The air was fresh and sweet, carrying aromas of flowers and spices.

She walked among the people and they gathered around her like a magnet. Little girls hugged her and tugged at her skirt. Young men nodded greetings while others stopped to chat. She had warmth and charm and she was exquisitely beautiful. Her name was Leel.

Where she came from was a mystery, but soon she was adored by all. In time, the people of Jewell were proud to claim Leel as one of their own. Over the past year they grew to know and love her, and they relished in her goodness. No one seemed to know why this being with the strange name was so special, only that to a person, they valued her presence among them.

How could they guess Leel was a stranger, not only to them, but to their planet, a woman so attractive, so feminine, so comely in her human coverings. And she was also possessed of the internal workings of the human — lungs, kidneys and heart.

But Leel's brain was designed as a circuit center of her existence on earth. Green and pulsating within, it compiled and centered the data she was collecting over each of her Earth-days. This information would assist the eventual Daxonian takeover — climate, atmospheric changes, and information about Earth's waters were recorded in a steady stream. This circuit center clicked continuously, imprinting the transmissions while she slept and while she was awake.

It was now approaching the end of Leel's complete year on Earth. She was passing to the end of her fourth season, her mission almost complete. Her time on the planet was coming to an end. She felt the signals inside getting stronger and knew it was time to go the meadow and wait.

But the prospect of leaving saddened her, for she had grown close to these humans around her. These feelings had not been anticipated, especially by her, when she felt overwhelmed by the strange urgings from deep inside her human heart. But she should have seen it coming. Hadn't she wept when she happened upon the gold and red trees of the Scottish Highlands?

Or when she experienced sudden fits of laughter at a baby's silly expression? Or delighted at the taste of delectable food...or basked in the closeness of others huddling for warmth when the November winds blew?

Yes, she thought, the Earth-year was over. It was time for her mate Tark to bring her home. The past days she felt her earth body weakening and knew she had but a short time. She knew in time she would wither and die like her fellow creatures she had lived among. When her false exterior eventually disintegrated, her alien form would live but weeks in the foreign air.

Before she left for the rendezvous, she turned and smiled one last time at the ones she had come to know and love. The heart they had given her was a real one and she was able to feel sadness and joy with its great power. The part of her brain that was not computerized, allowed her to think and to know, and to feel. Because of that, her senses were burning and alive. It was strange, but wonderful— this connection between heart and mind. She did not want the feelings to end.

In the meadow surrounded by acres of green grass, Leel waited. The pulsating in her brain became stronger as a green glow cast its light against a nearby rock. The ship was on schedule. It dropped from above as planned, its green laser beam focusing in to make the connection. There was no time to waste, for the crew was not able to sustain Earth's atmosphere.

Should a delay occur or if an earth-being took notice of his presence, Tark was fitted in the skin and likeness of the male human species. Reddish hair topped his head and also covered the lower portion of his face. They called it a "beard." Like Leel, he was made to look strong and handsome to the human eye, her counterpart, down to his set of twinkling brown eyes. Also, like Leel, his human form was temporary: he had limited time before he too would begin to wither, perhaps only weeks.

The mother ship hovered above until the connection to Leel was secure and for a short time she was rendered motionless. She was caught in the beam until the lower door slid open and

Tark was tossed to the Earth's floor with a thud. There, he rose and released Leel from the beam, setting her free.

The two mates stared at each other for long moments until Tark held out his hand. Leel ignored the gesture, using hers instead to touch Tark's face. Running her fingers through his soft hair, she then felt his beard and gave it a playful tug and laughed. He froze. Under her gentle touch and calm gaze he became uneasy inside-a stirring that was new and strange and wonderful and scary. The human heart, he wondered? And maybe that part of the brain Daxonian machinery could not reach.

"Come with me," she said, taking his hand in hers.

She led him to the edge of the meadow. Tark's eyes scurried about, out of his control, bouncing hither and thither in the confusing brilliance of the surroundings. Leel pointed to apple orchards and rows of purple lilac bushes. He looked out over acres of lush grass and felt the wind's caress, and the warmth of the sun beating down on his human skin.

Tark thought of his race, of his planet so desolate, so cold and bare — just miles of grey sand and darkness.

He turned to Leel and noticed a softness in her being. Her eyes did not dart about nervously, but gazed serenely first in one place, then another. He forced his eyes to do the same and soon came to realize, and then to savor, this calmness, this peace, he had never experienced. It caused him to falter...to sway and almost collapse. Leel steadied him and led him down a short path to tiny cottage with a thatched roof that she called "home." She proudly displayed her few possessions, colorful plants, a bed and a quilt that was billowy and soft to the touch.

Two strange life-forms ran inside the cottage and scampered near her feet. Tark backed away in fright. "Dogs," she explained laughing and knelt down to their level where they nuzzled her neck with playful affection.

Nearby, the crew was growing impatient. Green laser beams flashed about trying to locate the two, attempting to make the connection to bring them back to the ship. There was little time, for the ship was on a computer lock-in schedule and within minutes the signal would alert them to depart. Tark ignored the frantic searching beams. He was overwhelmed by the beauty of Earth and the strange emotions he saw radiating from Leel. As the beams came in closer, she pulled him close and spoke, looking directly into his eyes. "I will not go with you," she whispered frantically. "I have but a short time left on Earth and I know I will die. But I must take this gift of human life and live it to the fullest. I have experienced life as it should be."

Tark listened as Leel described the oceans of earth. "Bodies of water as far as the eye can see," she breathed, "home to beautiful animals, magnificent creatures called whales and dolphins. The ocean is alive and has moods like the humans...anger and fury...contentment."

She told him about the sky over the waters, sometimes hovering menacing and strong, sometimes pale and quiet.

He was still as Leel spoke of sacred landscapes-of flowing rivers and streams that gave way to new life and arched stripes of colorful mist that painted the sky after a storm. "A Rainbow," she said.

Tark tried to imagine such bodies of water and the beauty she described, but the concepts were as strange and foreign to him as the joy, longing, and love she explained were part of human emotions that were openly displayed here. "I feel them. I know I can never return."

A strange look came over Leel's face and Tark saw odd drops of water flow downward from the corners of her eyes.

Both knew the data she had collected would be returned to the Highest Order and used, not to learn and to borrow, but for Daxonians to come down and ravage and steal and take all from Earth for their own. They were testing new ways to sustain Earth's atmosphere and once they received the data from Leel, it would not be long before they would invade. Both knew it when Leel left on her mission. Back then it meant nothing- just a mission set forth for the ultimate survival of their own.

She told Tark she believed then that taking from the weird looking Earth creatures would be an easy task, but she hadn't been prepared for the goodness and hope of the kind humans she encountered when she arrived. And the beauty. No one had prepared her for the site of luxurious vast bodies of water that covered the planet. Humans were working feverishly to protect them, for only recently had they discovered their importance for life and continued survival. Daxonians, Leel said, would have to look elsewhere in the galaxies for their answers.

"I will stay," Tark told her. "I, too, will die a slow and sure death as my outer form withers in this foreign air. But I must see the oceans you speak of. I want to see the rivers and streams, and — yes — the rainbows that paint colors across the sky."

Tark and Leel walked out to the meadow and saw the flashing beams above them. They fell flat to the ground. Inch by inch they crawled, stopping to rest under a tree, hoping to escape being noticed by the green laser lights.

Their ship could wait no longer. The light-beams diminished and without making a sound the ship vanished. It would return to Daxon, but without the information they had been expecting. Tark mused in whispers about the livid anger from the Highest Order, how his anger would bellow and resonate across the galaxies.

Tark and Leel looked at each other and smiled.

They rose from the ground and began walking. Hand-in-hand they headed west. Evening would soon be upon them and there was no time to waste. The canvas sky was brilliant, painted in tints of purple, pink and orange. Leel brought Tark up to the top of a bluff that overlooked the river. She pointed ahead to the blinding array of exploding colors before them. The sky was on fire. It was a magnificent sunset, the first of Earth's many wonders she wanted to share.

The Goodbye Place

Middle Plains, Nebraska- 1977.

It was an ugly town; ugly buildings; boring people. At least to Jesse. How anyone could refer to it as anything else was beyond his imagination. Noticing the darkening skies, his eyes swept the length of Oak Street and the late autumn storm descending upon the small Nebraska town. In minutes sheets of harsh wet wind assaulted his position full on. But his face didn't waver from its force. He sat perched and unmoved high atop a cement wall, kicking his legs methodically to no distinct rhythm.

He was only sixteen but already beginning to show the signs of approaching manhood. Honey-colored peach fuzz sprouted in patches on his chin. His once-awkward body with spindly limbs were now defined in hard lines and contours. Once unsteady as a two-day-old calf, he now moved purposefully in long, clear strides.

"Goodbye boring town!" he yelled, his words caught in the expulsion of frosty breath before dying in the wind. "I'm leaving you today!"

Jesse was running away from a town that he thought was slowly killing him, a town that stifled his creativity and dampened his spirit. He blamed this town for this and could never forgive it.

He let his eyes wander over the brown brick buildings and surveyed the people with cynicism. Plain folk, he thought, plump and dowdy with their scrawny runny-nosed kids with banged-up knees. He scrutinized the street up and down with its weedy front yards, its rusty cars up on blocks—cars that would never run again blocking the sun of flowerbeds gone to seed, flowers that would never have a chance to grow. The men all looked the same, Jesse thought. Tired-looking robots in visor caps and faded overalls wearing worn boots caked with layers of dried Nebraska mud.

He didn't belong here. He never did.

Jesse was heading west to Hollywood, California. The place where folks dressed with style. A town filled with pretty women and sleek, fast cars. He'd seen pictures, sharp color pictures in the movie magazines he bought at Milt's Drug Store. Julie Christie. Warren Beatty. And his favorite, Mick Jagger. These were people, beautiful people, all living in a dreamy world of palm trees and city lights, a fantasy land, somehow real, of movie theaters and shopping centers the size of football fields.

His mother exploded in rage when she first discovered the magazines Jesse had hidden in the back corner of his closet. She yelled at him for days calling them a wasteful pile of junk. "What are you going to learn from these?" she screamed.

"How to add and subtract? History? Tell me one good thing that comes from buying this trash!"

He knew not to answer her. Not when she was in that state, when her face turned scarlet and the veins of her neck jutted in and out, and got worse with each reprimand. He knew to let her go on until she looked into his eyes and knew her child understood. Because she read those magazines cover-to-cover, too, he knew, and maybe shared his dreams. His mother also admired the famous familiar faces of the people in the beautiful town.

"It won't be long now," he yelled again to the wind, as if the Golden State could hear his taunting promise over two thousand miles away.

Every passing day had been one day closer to his escape. And now, today, the wait was over. He had finally saved enough money to buy his bus ticket out. Jesse was going to California. He would become a rock star — a legend in the minds and hearts of millions, as he was already in his own. For his part, his every breath would be devoted to his music and his fans. "Jesse!" they would scream when he was out on stage — begging for just a glance, an acknowledgment from him. And if they were lucky, his autograph.

His eyes cleared and once again wandered across the buildings of his own town. Once more he tried to find something, anything even remotely handsome in any of it. Something, some sight, some place that would be worth remembering. Nothing, he thought, shaking his head.

He looked up Oak Street to Lou and Emma's Café with its green exterior with white borders, its walls chipped and flaked, its front door that hung at an angle. No, he thought, oddly thinking of the bell that welcomed the patron into the cozy heat on days such as today. He stared at the windows which were patched with large squares of cardboard, half to cover the cracks in the glass and half to tell the passerby what was on the menu. Even so, the heat inside never escaped and the menu never changed.

He read the words aloud to himself, fighting his fondness, "Chile and Cornbread, $1.29. Emma's Cheddarburger cooked only as Emma can make 'em— fried on a griddle in a half-ton of grease." He sighed. "Goodbye Lou and Emma."

He saluted.

Frowning and resolute he turned away. "I have forgotten you already," he said as a fresh gust of vanguard wind blasted his face and teared up his eyes.

The clouds turned blackish-purple and Jesse knew that the storm would be a nasty one.

"Jesse, you best be getting down off that wall!" Fat Clara called out to him. "Bad weather is on the way."

He signaled assent to her as he fought a smile at the loose skin under her arms jiggling as she shook her fist in the air. Then he watched her large behind waddle back and forth as she walked away. Safe now, he let loose his smile. She was truly a Middle Plains woman-big and hearty, he thought. He knew, as all these sturdy women did, that Clara worked her fingers to the bone—baking, washing clothes, raising six children. He shook his head. Fat Clara and the people of Middle Plains would live and die here, Jesse knew that for sure. They had a life here and they had each other. He supposed they were happy, proud to call this home. He guessed everyone was happy. Everyone except Jesse.

But in a few hours, all that would change. He would be free, free of these dilapidated buildings and free of the same faces he was forced to confront day after day. His bus was leaving at six and he wouldn't miss it. Even if he had to crawl the two miles in the rain and mud, he would be there. Once he crossed the state line he would never return. Jesse planned to erase this part of his life-to start over, and live his life as it was meant to be lived.

He thought about his mother. She would cry when she realized he was gone. But she would have Stretch Cooper, her Clark Gable, to console her. He was the mechanic who repaired his mother's car, but Jesse knew there was much more to his mother and Stretch's relationship. He didn't know what to think of it. He guessed it was okay. Besides he was on his way West. He was happy Stretch was hanging around his mother now, after his dad had left so many years ago. Yes, he thought, good that Stretch would watch over his mother and keep her safe.

Jesse thought about his mother and smiled. She was a good woman, young inside. She loved rock and roll. Her favorites were "Three Dog Night" and "The Stones." Jesse recalled with a laugh that day school let out early and he walked in the house unexpected only to hear Mick Jagger screaming "Honkey-Tonk Woman" from the speakers and rattling the windows. And when he walked in, he saw his mother shaking it—dancing, jumping, and singing. He watched in amazement until she gyrated around and froze in mid-jump when she saw him. But Jesse immediately went into Jagger's character, and strummed his notebook like a guitar, singing the words with her. Then they danced. Afterwards she laughed as Jesse had never heard her laugh before, not even with Stretch, and then went about her chores. They listened to music together from that day on and sometimes danced, but never as wildly.

Another blast of wind hit and he wiped the dust from his brow and eyes. She was a kind mother, he knew, but the blood-bond between them was not enough to make him stay.

Hard drops of rain stung his cheeks. Drenched, shivering, defiant, Jesse would leave only when he called it. He played by his own rules, not those of the descending storm.

Minutes passed until out of the corner of his eye he thought he saw a flutter of a skirt. For some reason this brought Fonda Freeman to mind. He grimaced.

"Goodbye Fonda Freeman. If I never hear your name again it will be too soon!" he sang.

Fonda, he frowned again, if this storm blows her home to the ground she would crawl out of the rubble and walk, knees knocking to find him. She would stand in his space, try to kiss his cheek-her dagger braces scraping against his skin.

She had been in love with Jesse since the first time he tried to kiss her in the school playground. They were only ten back then, but she was pretty, with red hair and a splatter of freckles across her upturned nose. From that day on, Fonda had lusted after Jesse's body. She would do anything for him. Jesse couldn't escape.

He told her off once, saying she looked like the female toads at Elk Pond. But she smiled and opened her mouth for a French Kiss. He even went so far as to fix his cousin Albert up with her, but Albert returned the next day and gave him a black eye. "Returning the favor," he told Jesse, "All she talked about was you." From then on, he tried to ignore her, but she always seemed to crop up wherever he went. And when she didn't, he'd feel weird, that maybe something happened to her. He could set his watch by her though.

"In a few years you will be begging Fonda to go out with you," his mother told him. "Look at her red hair, Jesse. Her beautiful green eyes."

All Jesse felt was sick. He envisioned her standing before him years down the road, in his space, even as she matured to womanhood. And anyway, now her braces blinded him when the light bounced off them in a certain way. But his mother had a point about those green eyes, he thought, her green eyes that almost reflected himself—even if it was him screwing up his eyes at her with disgust at her relentless pursuit.

He turned away from his thoughts briefly and screamed at the wind, stronger now and blowing more determined. "I will never want Fonda!"

But his thoughts returned to her, with the same disgust. Fonda wouldn't let me be, he thought, she was everywhere. He remembered his birthday party last year when his mother invited her (along with every man, woman and child in town). Who all jumped out and scared and mortified him when he walked in the door. His immediate reaction was to turn and run, but a sea of tentacle arms without bodies seemed to reach out and grab him, pulling him in.

In the mass of human faces, Fonda found his. She eased her way across the room, ducking, bending, slinking sideways through the crowd until she reached him. Moving in close to Jesse's side she slipped her hand into his and grasped it. He felt her clammy skin and it took every ounce of strength not to yank his hand from hers. He knew if he did, she would make a scene.

Fonda pressed in closer and closer. She lifted his arm, encircling it around her shoulders. He left it there until he looked about the room and felt that all eyes were staring at him and Fonda, especially his mother's—her smile sweet and tender in understanding. Jesse began to hyperventilate. Palpitations overtook him, his heart skipped, and his breathing gave way to short, rapid breaths. Faintness enveloped his body. He was angry at himself for losing control. All this because of Fonda. He had never felt that strangely sick before.

And yet she persisted to bat her eyes and nuzzle her face below his chin. Jesse's arms began to tingle and his legs and knees grew weak. Before he lost control of his legs completely and he was her captive Jesse could only think one rational though—run! He had to run, to get away from her spider grip or he would die right there in front of everyone. He pushed her and ran, each long step felt like slow motion-all the while shaking the numbness from his limbs. Out the door, across the yards he ran in giant strides, until he could breathe freely once again.

He took a few gulps of the refreshing wind as a shiver ran through his body. He felt as if he exhaled her essence once and for all into the now mounting storm.

"Good Riddance, Fonda!" he whispered, feeling a measure of calm and relief Never would he have to run from her again.

Jesse checked his watch. Two hours to freedom. He jumped off the ledge and started walking toward the station. He picked up speed and sprinted across muddy roads. The black clouds opened and hard rain chased him, following the boy over open fields. Freezing pellets battered his skin, slowing his momentum and Jesse had to hold his arms in front of his face, to protect himself from the battering force.

Slipping and sliding in mud-pockets along the way, he ran to Elk Pond for cover. Jesse entered the pond area where hundreds of branches from the trees intertwined above, forming arches, moving arches constructed of bony fingers that clicked and moved about with each gust of wind. The dome created by the many branches formed a protective ceiling which blocked out the outside world. The dome of trees over the pond prevented most of the pounding rain sheets from entering this magical misty enclosure, allowing drizzle to surround the boy.

Elk Pond. His salvation, the only place where Jesse felt at peace. At the pond Jesse could dream and verbalize these dreams. He could talk out loud about his plans for the future, and nobody would laugh. Here he could try out songs he had written and sing them to the waterfowl who gathered about him at attention to listen to his concerts and hear them without mock or malice. These were his true fans. His voice never wavered here, but echoed strongly through the trees. The birds seemed to realize this was Jesse's on-going audition, his apprenticeship before launching into his career that would someday place him in arenas where swarms of fans would one day be at his feet below the stage, demanding encore after encore from their god, their idol.

In the summer months Jesse swam in the pond water, oblivious to the algae and moss that clung to his body as he splashed and paddled about in the green muck. In winter he lay flat in the snow looking up at the dome above. Flurries that escaped through the branches covered Jesse's face then dissolved to winter water in a matter of seconds. It was a place of wonder and beauty in the blustery winter months. It was a place where Jesse could talk, laugh and cry—and expose his heart.

But Elk Pond in the late autumn was his favorite. He liked to write songs sitting on the blanket of colorful leaves that lay scattered across the ground. Burning leaves around the area threw off intoxicating smells that filled his senses. Smoldering piles in the surrounding yards could get Jesse high—for he reveled in the swirling pungent smoky smell of the heady mixture of birch, oak and pine.

It was fitting that this magical place be his final stop. The Goodbye Place that Jesse visited before he left on his life's journey.

He sat at the base of a tree catching his breath, then checked his watch again. Only thirty minutes left and he would be gone—leaving all behind in his dust. White mist and the dense fog began to lessen the boy's visibility. The branches swayed to let in more of the sheets of rain.

"Hey!" he yelled, testing his voice strength, but his words seemed to sputter and die just inches from his face in the mist that surrounded him.

"Splash!" Jesse heard a rock hit the water just a few yards away.

"Who threw that?" Jesse said quietly as if to himself as he tried in vain to pinpoint the source through the mist, yet he knew someone was there just out of sight skipping stones across the water.

"Who's there?" His voice broke, swallowing back the words. Jesse's heart began to pound thinking he saw a form in front of him at the pond's edge.

He got up and stumbled forward but had to put his arms forward to keep from walking into the pond or into a tree. He blinked several times but could not seem to clear his vision.

Again a splash, a rock tossed into the water. Jesse fell to his knees. He crawled, inching closer to the pond, using his hands as a guide. They clawed the wet ground as he instinctively made his way forward. Squinting, creeping on all fours he saw what looked like a man. The husky form sat with his back to Jesse. It seemed transparent, for Jesse swore he saw through it to the other side of the pond. The boy sat staring at the vision afraid to approach.

"Jesse" the figure bellowed. The haunting twangy voice was deep, mellow, and somehow familiar. A man, his hair back and glossy. Jesse heard the jingle of chains that appeared to hang from his neck.

"You are here to say goodbye." The rich drawl could only belong to one man, Jesse knew, but he was gone from this world months ago. A beloved figure leaving a mourning public.

Jesse tried to answer but his words stuck to his throat and only a gurgle escaped. He tried to speak again, this time finding strength in his words. "You're..."

"I am," the voice mocked, booming and rich.

Jesse shook, fear creeping through his limbs, recognizing the voice, the figure, the presence. But as soon as he thought it, he knew the man was departed from a world that bade him a tearful goodbye.

Why would he be here? In Nebraska? Jesse wondered. Was it Elk Pond? Its magic?

"This isn't...Memphis," the boy said out loud, his voice still awestruck. How cruel a mistake, Jesse thought, for such a great man to be at such a wrong-junctioned whistle-stop on his way through the white light.

"This is your Memphis, son. Your home. Your roots."

"Not mine," the boy corrected. "My roots were never planted. I'm going West to be a star."

"A star?" The voice chuckled. "You have been living here with the stars. It is their lights shining inside you. They are your roots- the seeds of your soul."

"Hah!" the boy spat. But the haunting voice jabbed at him through the mist. He threw a rock in the figure's direction and it whizzed right through, landing with a splash.

"The waters from this pond run through your veins....your memories have been spawned. You will take it with you, Jesse. All of it."

Jesse laughed. He was trying to erase it already.

" You can't run. It is only when you open your heart to their goodness...to your humble beginnings that your songs will flow. When it is time, your soul and all that it holds, will be there to guide you."

As he heard the words, the branches above cracked and lay back like the Red Sea allowing the storm to rage in. Jesse was soaked in seconds, immersed in mud-oblivious to everything around him but the words of the sayer.

His timidness dissolved—his voice now steady. "How do you know this?" he asked. Irritated by the silence he raised his tone. "Hound-Dog Man!"

The downpour cleared the mist and now he could see clearly to the pond. "When will it be time?" he demanded.

He rose and stumbled forward, determined to confront the southern wayward ghost. But the only movement were geese waddling around the pond and an occasional flutter of leaves from the tree branches.

There was no lurking presence. No mellow voice. Nothing, not even an indentation in the mud. Jesse realized he must have been talking to himself. Maybe he felt a little guilty for leaving, so his mind was just playing games, sending him off with words from a supposed spirit whose time to shine had passed.

He gathered himself together and kicked a hole in the mud, emphasizing his anger. Fool! Embarrassed, he made a promise with himself that he would never mention the event to anyone.

Yet, as he started to make his way out into the brunt of the storm on the way to town, the words nagged at him. He stopped at the edge of his canopy, walked back and let his eyes linger here and there as they swept the area. He nodded to his feathered friends, noticing for the first time, their humorous waddle and the way in unison, they honked a greeting. He closed his eyes and saw the faces, of his mother and Fonda. Jesse reached down, immersing his hand in the water, dallying in the magic and beauty of the Pond.

The dome branches finally parted all the way as if finally releasing their child from their protective care. He swiveled his hips and in a cocky swagger turned to leave. "Damn! He cursed, tripping over something laying in his path. "What is this?" he muttered, gathering two items in his hands. Jesse brushed them off. He cleaned them over and over with swift compulsive strokes as their shape and color became clear. He stared, motionless at his find.

Then the boy laughed and cried in a strange combined hysteria.

In the full and steady rain he ran home, clutching shoes— Blue Suede Shoes.

Eyes of the Gull

She was ninety-three today. Stella closed her eyes and rocked back and forth in the chair. "Happy Birthday to me," she sang softly as a single tear slid down her cheek. She knew what to expect from the staff. It was always the same: the stale cupcake with the half-burned candle and the off-key voices singing without harmony. And those around her who could still clap...would. Three whole minutes devoted to the celebration of her life. She rocked in the chair, patiently waiting for her three minute turn of attention, in her otherwise drab existence.

Her room at the Palm Nursing Home in Los Angeles was stifling. Particularly so on a hot July afternoon with the air conditioners idle and mute. Instead, two old green fans on each end of the room blew the stale, smoggy air from one wall to another almost gagging her with each pass. Even those few not beyond caring didn't seem to mind. They sat, staring, pausing to look up at the ceiling or down at the floor for variety. No one spoke. The only noise came from the honking of cars in the steady stream of traffic two flights below.

Stella took a deep breath and let her mind wander. She visited that part of her life with the most meaning, opening memories permanently etched in her brain. She was back at the ocean, in the tiny coastal town. From the wharf she gazed out on the colorful armada of fishing boats as she tasted the salt spray and was warmed by the steam of her cup of chowder on her unlined face. The sights and sounds and smells intoxicated her.

Sea otters splashed and played, the sea lions barked from their flat rocks and the waves crashed on the shore. All combined into music, her music. Stella walked out to the old wooden pier, her eyes squinting in the sun. But they were wide open, searching. She saw the boat, then him. He was standing at the pier's end with a line of fish.

"Solomon!" Stella's face broke into a smile and her heart jumped.

Tall, burly, sunburnt Solomon. His black curly hair whipped about in the wind and he held out his arms to her, open and waiting. She heard his deep laugh and her legs led her body, running across the wooden planks in strong, youthful strides.

She ran into him with a thud, almost knocking him over the edge. He laughed louder and picked her up, twirling her around with a great and loving force. His green eyes sparkled like emeralds as he pulled her face close and kissed her. They lingered for hours at the end of the pier, holding hands, laughing, talking, making plans for their future.

The sun began to set over the blue waters. The two became quiet as the fiery ball dipped into the water as it lit a distant coastal mountain red. As the evening wore, the sky darkened until peppered with a blanket of crystal stars. They watched the seagulls flying freely under the glare of the moon and they talked. About life and love. And death.

Solomon told her he hoped for a long and happy life. But when he died, he said, he would return again. He pointed to a flock of gulls in the distance. He told Stella his reborn soul would be as free and as happy as the soaring bird.

Stella laughed. She looked out at the group of gulls and said they all looked the same. "How will I ever know which one is you?" she teased, smiling. Her smile waned when she studied his face and saw his seriousness.

"You'll know me because I'll be different from all the others," he replied. This time he smiled. "I will be the brightest of the lot—I'll have the most beautiful colored feathers in the world."

Solomon looked upward and singled out one gull flying low across the waves. He pointed to it. They watched him swoop down and catch a fish, then fly upward, and finally join the others on a distant rock.

Solomon, serious again, told Stella that if he went first, he would come for her. "We will fly the seas together," he said, "but only when you're able and ready to surrender your soul."

The years passed. Solomon and Stella married but had no children. Instead, she joined him on his fishing boat where they lived a happy and joyous life, strong and healthy. Their home was where they landed, the various colorful ports along the Pacific Coast. Their faces became lined and weathered from the sea and sun. While others were busy raising families, Solomon and Stella sailed the sea, gathering lifetimes of experiences. Over six decades, their love never wavered.

But then, time began stealing from them in bits and pieces. Solomon's health was failing and he grew weaker into his eighty-sixth year. Stella's heart died the moment Solomon's stopped beating. In a hollow daze, she went through the motions of his physical passing. She was alone, truly alone for the first time in her life.

She missed him more than she ever imagined. The days turned into weeks, the weeks into months. Every day Stella walked along the shore, searching—in the coldest of winds and darkest of skies.

"Solomon!!" she would yell to the sea's indifferent motions.

Her life became mere existence, her day-to-day motions zombie-like. With little money or treasures of her own, she ended up in the bare surroundings of a rundown home far from her beloved ocean. From moonlit currents to flashing neons off dirty brick, from salt air to stale carbon monoxide-lined overcrowded quarters she went. This was her life.

The charms and feel of the sea faded abruptly as the off-toned strains of her birthday melody crowded in on her mind. She opened her eyes to three nurses standing over her, white hats in hand, one of which held her birthday cupcake with flickering half-candle inches from her face.

"Happy Birthday," they exclaimed, song finished as the uneven sounds of clapping assaulted her ears.

"We have a surprise for you, Stella," the head nurse announced.

She stared back, blankly.

Page | 155

"Today, we're going to take you to the seashore to spend the day." What a cruel joke to play on an old woman, she thought.

"Come. We are going on an outing. And we know how much you love the water," the night nurse said, then added, "how many times have I heard you talking in your sleep?"

They dressed her in a sweater and put a scarf about her head. Within an hour Stella was sitting on the sand at the ocean's door in a folding chair while her three keepers gathered on a bench nearby, gossiping, smoking, and laughing among themselves. Good riddance, she thought, smiling and wiggling her toes until her shoes fell from her feet. She dug them deep into the warm sand, then pulled the scarf from her head and tilted her face to the sky, soaking in the sun's rays.

It was a glorious afternoon. The screams of laughing children were muffled by the pounding surf as it hit the water's edge. "Stella is happy," she heard one of nurses say. They talked about her as if she was invisible, a ghost-form seated just a few feet away.

In time she could sit still no longer. Stella rose and slowly began walking in the direction of the wooden pier in the distance.

"Don't go far!" she heard one scold.

She knew nothing could bring her back now.

Step-by-step, barefooted, she made her way across the burning sand. While her caretakers sat huddled together talking among themselves, Stella walked further and further away. She reached the pier and inched her way down toward the far end. Her feet were bleeding from the slivers of wood that she picked up along the way, but her mind was numb to all pain. She clung to the side rails and never once looked back.

A blue and orange fishing boat passed in the distance, wind chimes from the bait shop tinkled in the breeze, and a sea lion barked from a gathering of rocks. Stella inhaled deeply. Her first real breath in ten years, she knew. Her mind suddenly became focused and clear. Tall waves crashed under the wooden planks and Stella held the rail tightly. She stood quietly, her hair flying freely in the wind and looked out to sea, searching.

"Solomon!" she tried to call, but her voice was raspy and weak. "My soul...it is ready."

Tears flowed fast and furious down her cheeks, unchecked. Her eyes clouded with moisture until suddenly the heat and light from two green sparkling stones clarified her vision. They stared, like emeralds they were, she thought, gasping. Her jaw dropped with the realization that these gems were eyes and shone from the most magnificent bird she had ever seen in her life. A grand bird, a seagull, perched on a post just inches from her face.

Stella backed away to get a better view. This gull was different from the others, she thought, his feathers like satin and hued in crimson, grey and turquoise. She reached out her hand and the gull flapped his powerful wings as if in greeting, then flew upward and circled her head. She watched as he did an air dance for her in the sky out over the sea. The beautiful gull performed freely for her, swooping down toward her, then shooting out in the other direction. As the bird approached her and she saw his green emerald eyes again, her body froze.

Back and forth, again and again, towards her then away it came, as if beckoning her out to the water. Wherever it flew, it turned its head back to her and stared. The world was a blur to her but for the clear and constant and intense eyes of her gull. Decades lifted from Stella's tired body. She was young, vibrant once again. She leaned out farther from the edge of the pier now, dangerously. Feelings of power and love flowed through her veins at last. At last she released the force that had anchored her soul for so long. Free! She was free to roam the skies, consumed by a love so powerful it would last all eternity.

"Stella! Stella!" the frantic cries came. The sun had long set and the evening tides were washing up on shore. "Where are you Stella?"

The nurses ran up and down the pier for a third and fourth time searching for her while the police continued to search the coast in both directions. But there was no sign of the old one. She had vanished. The worst scenario had happened, they all thought: It was dark. Poor Stella had fallen over the edge and drowned. Fearing the worst — that she had finally washed up with the evening tide — searchers used flashlights under the pier, poking into every crevice. No luck.

Finally, with nowhere else to look, they left with sorrowful hearts.

Many hours passed. The moon rose and shone brightly over the waters and a calmness settled upon the bay. The sea lions sat peacefully on the flat rocks and clusters of stars twinkled above like diamonds. Under the light of the midnight moon, two gulls flew. They were beautiful gulls, strong and colorful. They circled, swooped and rose toward the sky as if dancing an aerial ballet. The sea lions and otters watched from below as the birds performed. It was a magical sight — a union of two souls united at last under a blanket of crystal stars.

Life in the Freezer

Amy first greeted the town of Timber Bay in a twenty degree below icy morning wind. Her cries pierced the early morning air outside the small hospital, her wails seeming to harmonize with the wind into an at once mournful and joyful whine above the barren trees. Her cries were an announcement of birth in this remote stretch of Arctic land battered by persistent blunt forces of winter storm and ocean gale. The town was isolated — the only way in or out was by a bi-weekly float plane delivering goods.

The child fussed, flailing her arms, searching frantically for focus, until her eyes locked upon a fuzzy image — a kind face hovering in her line of vision. The face's voice had a gentle sound, a voice so soft, so intimate and reassuring that the newborn's screams hushed to a whimper.

At that moment, Lillian knew she and her daughter had joined souls, were united as one. An invisible cord connected them, one stronger than the one the doctor had cut just moments before, separating them. It would be a powerful alliance, Lillian knew, one that scared her. She wondered if other new mothers felt the same.

This connection was made all the stronger by her realization that it was just the two of them. Amy's father had run off right after Lillian announced that she was expecting. She once again heard his meek words ring in her ear in the hush of the hospital room, "I'll stay if you want." She was angry still. "No, Charles," she had replied resolutely, "you don't sound like you are fighting to be part of this. I know you want to take that job in the States. We won't hold you back." She was already thinking of her and her Amy as a team then, as she looked away from his face, so disgusting to her. His simpering look — one of relief, not thanks. His foot was already half out the door.

She could have made a scene that day, dragging him back to meet his responsibilities. She could have demanded that he stay and be part of their lives. But that's not how she wanted it, a man holding his child out of duty, staring down at her with indifferent eyes. No, Lillian decided, she would become both mother and father to her child. She would raise her to be strong, while guiding her with gentleness and compassion. "Good luck to you Charles," she had said to his back, and he was gone. She never knew, or cared, whether he heard them.

When Lillian brought Amy back to the two-room cabin she called home, she spoke softly to the child who slept in her arms. "I'm sorry, little girl. I wish I had pretty pink roses to welcome you home."

For a moment, Lillian wished she and Amy were returning to a real neighborhood, the kind with big square houses and sidewalks full of children riding bikes on a warm, sunny afternoon. Lillian had always yearned to be part of a teeming community filled with families, dogs, and station wagons — with movie theaters, supermarkets, fancy restaurants, and shopping centers.

Their town was so small it hardly qualified as a dot on the map. It hosted eleven months of winter only briefly respited by a docile spring of a few weeks of melting snow. Spring. It was only a cold runoff of water making its way through mosaics of thickets and forests.

Their town's rambling shorelines never seemed to end. These provided a backdrop for deep fjords and bays. There were no roads to speak of — no avenues that connected the communities — only the plane and an occasional barge that floated in and out through the long winter months.

Lillian's folks were born here, and their parents as well. The family owned "Murphy's," a cannery near the shore. The two thousand-square-foot warehouse had been in the family for over seventy-five years. Though small, with only a few canning lines and walk-in coolers, it supported a dozen employees, whose duties included smoking and curing fresh seafood, hand packing it and shipping it out on a barge to other isolated towns.

One day it would be hers, Lillian knew, her legacy, having worked there on and off since her early teens. Now, her parents were teaching her the management side. Under their careful guidance she was learning the business inside and out, so that when her turn came, Murphy's Cannery would continue to thrive, producing over one thousand units each day.

Amy's birth was a cause for celebration at the cannery. When Lillian brought her to work for the first time, the employees fussed over the chubby-faced baby bundled in a soft wool blanket.

"Let Grandma hold her," her mother demanded, clutching for the infant, only to then hold her above her head. "Take a look around, Baby Amy," she said, "soon you'll be working here with us." She yelled at the workers on the line, "Keep a chair open!"

"What if she doesn't want to work here? What if she wants to go away to school?" Lillian found herself saying in a tone to tease, but with a message that was unequivocally firm.

Her mother gave her a strange look, like she had lost her mind. "Why would she want to go away to school? She can be schooled here. She'll have a job waiting for her. Murphy children stay close to home."

Lillian exhaled and said nothing. She knew that when Amy was older, she would be expected to join the team. The expectations were already laid out for her and it saddened Lillian to think that this town would be all she would ever know. No one questioned a Murphy about their dreams or ambitions. It was expected that they would continue on in the cannery.

No one had ever asked Lillian what she wanted to become when she reached adulthood. She had dreams of leaving, of experiencing what life was like in the outside world. But Lillian was afraid to speak up. It was as if a map of her life had already been drawn after birth. No one wondered if she was happy. If anyone had expressed interest, she would have told them. "I hate living my life in a freezer."

So, Lillian buried her feelings, and kept them buried. It was her secret that she found her work at the cannery boring. So monotonous. Daily, she put herself in a trance to get through it. When others on the line talked to her about their lives, Lillian stared through them, watching their mouths move, hearing nothing.

She felt she was not there by choice, but appointment. And guilt. Ever since she could remember, her parents told her, "Thank God we have you to take over when the time comes." She felt she had been weaned on, "What would we do without you?" And all its variations. She had been born to carry on the tradition as the natural replacement when the time came. It was her name that was special, the continuing link in the line to keep the company around. She lived inside a continually shaken dome toy, forever invisible in the falling flakes of fake snow.

To make matters worse, Lillian knew her mother already had plans for her granddaughter. But not this time. Not with her Amy, she vowed. She had other intentions for her child. Early in her pregnancy Lillian decided to break the chain.

There was another world beyond this isolated and frozen outpost, an exciting world of unlimited possibilities — people to meet, lands to explore. Lillian kept her plan a secret from her parents. In her mind, her plan was in motion. Her child would leave as a young woman, perhaps to one of the multitude of good colleges out there. If Lillian didn't take charge, Amy would be stuck in a life chosen for her, behind iceberg walls and unmovable mountains. She would exist like her mother, under a dome of cold and white.

As time passed Amy grew from a happy baby into a wide-eyed inquisitive toddler. Lillian would bundle her up in a thick padded snowsuit, with a scarf and mittens for their daily walks. And Amy would observe the natural world around them. She might point out a baby hawk peering at them from a branch or an eagle diving for fish in the salmon stream. "Look at the big dog" Lillian recalled her saying once. When she turned around Amy was giggling, petting a moose that had wandered into their yard.

Her daughter made friends with mountain goats and even baby wolverines. She decided it would be safer for her to run about down by the shore where she could keep an eye on her daughter as she frolicked, tossing stones about the sand.

One day while Amy played at the shore, Lillian sat next to her on a flat rock, staring out at the icy sea. She saw the blue-white glaciers that stood in the distance like giant blocks in the water. Sea Otters rested on platforms below. The crashing waves grated on her ears. She longed for the melody of soft waves, lapping, rhythmic, tropical gatherings of water that made their way across a beach of beige sand–the kind that left tiny shells and other surprises for children to discover and collect.

"One day you will visit a sea that is warm and gentle, that helps boats get to their destinations, and doesn't cause such fury and destruction," she whispered to her daughter.

It was an angry sea that day, every day, one that frightened even the locals with its strength and fury, and seemed to take glee from the fear. It thrived on stormy gales, taking delight in its sporadic rampages. She blamed the raging sea for much of her unhappiness, deciding it was at fault for their isolation.

As the seasons passed, her daughter didn't seem bothered by their surroundings, but thrived, growing up a healthy child, robust and strong. Amy had many playmates from the few families, and they would gallivant in the drifts of snow and make silly-looking snowmen with carrot noses and black olive eyes. They slid down hills with sleds made from squares of torn cardboard.

Her daughter's wonderland remained her mother's hell. She would watch her daughter playing, seemingly oblivious to the surging blasts of cold air whipping up around the cabins and teasing the icicles hanging off rooftops packed with several inches of fresh snow. And her grudge against this cold jail would simmer.

Lillian obtained a home-schooling certificate and taught her daughter how to read and write. Lillian was preparing her, showing her pictures from magazines, describing places many miles away. "These are palm trees and they sway in a warm breeze. These skies are deep blue and when it rains, the rain is warm and gentle across the land. It is the most beautiful place in the world."

Amy would listen, wide-eyed, straining to imagine how others lived. Lillian told her about the desert's hot sands that stretched for miles. "The desert is warm during the day but cool at night. People say that when the sun sets over the sand the sky becomes full with different colors. It is one of the prettiest sights you will ever see."

On Saturday afternoons, mother and daughter would go for rides through the lowland coastal areas to explore fjords and winding passageways. They would park at the bottom of a hill and walk up to a crest where they'd stop and look over vast areas of white snow in the endless horizon.

Lillian remembered the day Amy heard the rustling noise. Just yards away were two brown bear cubs scampering around a tree. "Mom, look. They're so cute." Amy started running towards them only to stop when she heard the fear in her mother's voice. "Stay away. They're just babies. Their mother will be back. We don't want to be anywhere near when she comes," Lillian warned.

She grabbed Amy's arm and pulled her down the hill. She knew it could be minutes before the mother bear appeared and it was not a place she wanted to find herself in.

"A mamma bear protecting her babies can be dangerous, Amy," Lillian explained on their way back. "She wouldn't understand you want to be friends with her babies, but might hurt you. She would hurt us if she had to, taking a stand against any outside force that might do her family harm.".

Over the following months Lillian and Amy tracked the bears. They drove as far as they could to the top and sat inside the truck watching the cubs play. "Why don't they run away?" Amy would ask.

"They're not ready to leave home yet. They have to learn how to survive. They have to know where to find berries and how to hunt the waters for fish." She explained as best she could that there would come a moment when the cubs would have the knowledge and would turn and take that first step away, instead of instinctively towards home.

As predicted, during the second spring, the cubs disappeared. Lillian drove her truck through the area and spotted the mother roaming about the drifts. She thought about the bear and about her own feelings as a mother and realized that there was not much difference between the two. There came a time when even the bear, a ferocious protector, had to say goodbye. A time when she saw those first small steps taken in another direction and there was nothing she could do. It was a moment when her young did not scamper back into her clutches, but instead ventured alone into the unknown.

Lillian knew the time was approaching when Amy would be leaving for school. It had always been looming in the future, but now was becoming more real and frightening with each passing day. It was easier to think about it when she knew she had time, years, left with her precious daughter. But as the years flew by, she watched Amy blossom into a young teenager, she felt an uneasiness stirring inside her. The promise she made stood in front of her, reminding her that the plan was real and approaching. Lillian knew she would have to be strong. She would soon have to open the door and show her the way, much like a cub on her way to an independent life.

"Are you sure about this, Mom? I wouldn't mind waiting. You'll be lonely without me."

Lillian wanted to answer, "My days will be empty without you, I want to have you next to me. Stay, so we can be silly together, so we can share clothes and make hot cocoa on lazy Sunday mornings."

Instead, she spoke the words that mothers say when it is time to let go. "Don't worry about me. I'll be fine. There's a whole world waiting for you out there."

The break would have to be clean and swift. She knew. It would hurt, like a second cutting of the life-cord. But she could see that her daughter was excited, ready to embark on an

Page | 165

extraordinary journey. She knew in her heart it was right. Amy was ready.

Whereas Lillian seemed to walk through her life with blinders, Amy seemed to take notice of all around her. She caught the look on her face when the moon shone across fresh snow making the flakes sparkle. She directed Lillian's attention to the bordering cliffs, amazed how they looked bathed in orange light as the sun went down behind them. It was Amy who asked how storm clouds formed, how tall were the snow-dipped mountains.

"You know, Mom," she said once, "I think this is the most beautiful place in the world." Lillian realized that Amy was taking with her memories that would hold her steadfast during her time away. She truly loved their town. Even the icy sea would be warm in memory.

When Lillian went to visit her own mother, she decided to tell her about Amy's plans. Surprisingly, her mother said, " I wish I could have done the same for you. I didn't have the courage to let you go. A mother's heart is a strange vehicle, Lillian. Sometimes it stalls, wondering which direction it should be headed. All it takes is courage to show it the way."

Lillian knew her home, much like the bear's den, would always be waiting. It was a comfort zone, where a child has learned to love and be loved.

Amy passed her eighteenth birthday. The day had come, one that Lillian had been waiting for and dreading. They sat at the kitchen table, her daughter read a list of last-minute things to pack. She had chosen a school in Florida and would be living in a dormitory with others her age.

Was she doing the right thing, Lillian wondered? She had taught her daughter to read and how to write. She taught her how to add and subtract and to paint imaginative landscapes. It was her hope that Amy had learned enough of life's lessons. For she would be walking towards a separate life now — pursuing her own interests, acting on her own desires.

Wait till she gets there, Lillian thought, studying her daughter. Let her startle them. Let them step back when they discover that her inner beauty even surpasses her outer radiance. Her humor and charm will astonish her future teachers and friends. Lillian was gifting them with her daughter; she was not arriving in fancy red bows, but wrapped in an aura of innocence...of wonderment. She was so accepting of others, so ready to inhale the new world around her.

Lillian felt an alliance with the mother bear she had seen years ago. She knew that time would heal the emptiness and that her heart would beat strong once again. That she would look at her den as not an empty place, but one that had served a great purpose. A place of nurturing, of taking a helpless being and shaping them to be able to move through life hardy and self-reliant.

The plane had come to take her. Lillian stood facing her daughter. One more time she looked closely into her eyes. She searched for fear. She searched for regret. None was visible. Her child's eyes were steady, bright and eager. Lillian breathed a sigh of relief. For had there been a spark of dread—a hint of apprehension—she knew she would have pulled her back. The child she was sending off was a woman, brave and fervent.

"I'll be back, you know. Is there anything you want me to bring you?" Lillian hesitated. Then: "Pink Roses."

Amy climbed on to the steps of the plane and turned to her mother. Suddenly, there was more Lillian wanted to tell her. She wanted extra time. But her daughter was standing on the top step waving, ready to enter the plane.

Morning fog and flurries were between them and Lillian could not see her just yards ahead. She searched the area in front of her trying to catch a glimpse of her daughter's face before it turned to leave.

Lillian leaned in closer to the fence that stood between them. She peered into the foggy veil; her daughter's shape hazy before her eyes. Then, she heard her voice, as soft and reassuring as was hers to a wailing child many years ago. The daughter's

Page | 167

calming tone quieted the mother's anguish, letting her know the bond was still there, as strong as it was the first time they laid eyes upon each other.

"I love you Mamma Bear."

"I love you too!" Lillian's words dissolved in a gust of tempest wind.

"Grant her the wings," she whispered as the silver plane rose, then disappeared into the clouds. It was a brief farewell, but a notable moment that gave way to a young girl's parade of dreams.

Rhythm of Life

The whole clan filled the back room of the Cantina Restaurant comprised of all four of Harry Lewis' sons with their wives and children. Tonight was Harry's night, and the family sat expectantly in their finery with gifts, each of his sons prepared with words to honor their father's eightieth birthday. It was all the more sweet for being unrehearsed when the youngest of Harry's grandchildren, six-year-old Susan, rose timidly, approached her Grandpa sitting at the head of the table and looked up to his grizzled face. In her tiny hand she toyed with a rumpled scribbled-upon piece of lined school paper. They room was quiet as she began to read. On the paper was a list explaining all the reasons she loved her grandpa. After rushing through it with cracking voice, she wrapped her arms around him and gave him a hug. Suddenly and spontaneously the older grandchildren followed her lead and converged on the surprised man, and his white hair and tweed coat was all arms and hugs and whispered words and tears.

Then it was time for each of the sons to stand and give tribute to Harry. Each in his own way said the unsayable–each thanked him in his own way for Harry's lifetime of commitment to them and expressed his gratitude. Susan's father, Ted, the onetime baby of the family, approached with something in his hand.

"Happy Birthday, Dad. We have a special gift for you," he said, handing his father a small gift. "Please accept this from all of us."

Harry unwrapped and opened it. Inside the small box was a blue pin in the shape of an anchor. The father and grandfather's eyes misted as Harry held the pin lovingly in his hand, turning it over and over, examining it. Then he nodded with a long sigh. "Thank you, my children."

"For the anchor of our family," Ted told him. "You've been there always for us. Like a rock. Tough, wise, loving to all of us."

Harry wiped his eyes with his sleeve and turned away for a second, then arose to applause and whistles as he acknowledged his family.

"Speech!" someone called out.

Harry considered this a moment. He cleared his throat, then spoke to the faces that stood before him.

"An anchor. Thank you again," he began, holding the pin up to his family. "There are many kinds of these, my children—heavy, iron ones that are pounded in place. Immovable, these kinds hold steadfast over time. But other anchors are lighter, and many of these invisible—grounded not out of duty but of desire. We all carry one of these throughout life."

"When I was a young man, engaged to be married to your mother, I suddenly had second thoughts about putting down my anchor, though I was taking steps towards a future with her. Being a youngster, I was scared. It wasn't easy making promises for a lifetime commitment," he smiled. "For one such as myself....so savvy, so full of verve, so full of himself with my bounce in my walk." Harry paused and looked to each of his sons in turn. "Yes, it would've been easy to bounce away in one foolish brazen stride and walk away." He looked down and toyed with the pin. "Back then great responsibilities were looming, sometimes I thought like a dark cloud. The boy in me wanted to run away and I almost listened to him. I wanted to run away to sea, work on a fishing boat, and sail the open seas, free from any obligations.

"But the man in me insisted I stay. Hell, I wanted to, knowing somehow despite my youth and stupidity that there just might be a rich life ahead of me. Oh, not in dollars," he smiled, then continued seriously, "but in the blessings of a loving wife and children—treasures from the heart that I would be eternally grateful for. The man was right. I have you to show for that.

"Throughout my marriage to your mother, Rose, that boy would impishly show up in my dreams and during times of difficulty urge me to pull that anchor chain loose and heave it over the side. I was overwhelmed at such times, the times of financial setbacks, the times of illness...the sad occasions of questioned or tempted fidelities." He stared over the room. "Yes, even Rose and I were young..."

The family laughed as Harry took a sip of wine.

"As all married men feel at times, I wanted to turn my back on all of it, to sail off with my buddies in a boat, see the world. That pesky boy would urge me to chart a course, to hit every loose port with its looser women, who would treat me like that youngster said I should be treated, like the king I most assuredly was, with no strings attached. But what did that youngster know?

"The man in me counseled me to stay, and I knew manhood would thrive and become stronger in me if I tried to overcome, and struggled for new triumphs. And, you know what, I did triumph a little day by day, all the while the man in me was growing. The man knew that loyalty worked, that it ensured and enhanced a little thing called devotion, and that as devotion grew, weaknesses wouldn't seem so bad to the ones you loved. He was right again." Harry inhaled a long breath. "You see, children, I was very anxious as a young married man and could've very easily followed that adolescent false path–that sideways jaunt—but instead I listened to the man, and chose to play it steadfast, to plant my roots and seed the soil. I stayed anchored," he said holding his pin up to his sons, then looked at them. "And I watched my garden flourish.

"But even the sturdiest anchors loosen over time. Children, for one thing, can sometimes cause great difficulty. You kids weren't any different. When your mother and I had you children, there were plenty of woes, problems that challenged me beyond my capabilities. Medical issues, school concerns, legal complexities. Oh, yes, raising four spirited boys took its toll. I was tired, weary, and often was convinced I was a failure as a father. Why, I'd ask myself, were my children entangled in such crises? Why was our family in constant distress? Many times I was tempted to turn my back, and that imp from my youth would rear his head and laugh. And I'd tell myself that I had enough money saved to buy a sturdy enough craft to sail away from here, to sail to hell and back. It sounded swell. I told myself that your mother, Rose, was the strong one anyway, she could take charge while the king in me took leave— to experience oneness—to aimlessly wander the waters.

"But once again, the man in me chose to stay. By now, the man had taught me that with hard work, discipline and love my sons would get through their troubled times." He smiled down at his children. "And, guess what? They did. And that with guidance they would one day come to see their way into the outside world, gracious and mindful. And they...you...have.

"When you children had your own children, it was an exciting time. By now I was firmly anchored, a landlubber, secure as I watched you with admiration as you all pondered each crucial decision. Many times I didn't agree with your paths, but the man knew enough to stay in the background. Each of you had problems that sometimes I thought even overshadowed my former albatrosses. So, how could I offer advice and direction when you came to me for it? I tried to help. I think I helped.

"But then your mother took ill. I watched her beautiful mind slip away by inches all the while knowing there'd come a day that all our faces would be strange to her." Harry paused and cleared his throat. "Suddenly I had the weight of the world on my shoulders. It was a heavy load to bear. That pesky rascal showed up again telling me there'd be plenty of caretakers willing and able to handle your mother. And he said I should back away from you children, and let all of you handle your own obligations to your families. The boy whispered in my ear to go away on a safari, worlds away. Why not? I was fit. I felt young. My boyish thoughts led to visions of jubilation, of meeting new people, seeing places I had only heard and read about.

"But the man in me marshaled the strength of years. I stayed, knowing I would be needed. And I was. And, besides, the boy and the man both knew there just wasn't much time left with my beloved Rose. The man in me thought that I might enlighten you with the wisdom I have learned. To help you understand certain ways of the world. And I did.

"And now dear children, I am in at eventide, still mourning with each passing day the loss of your mother. I know she would be proud of every one of you and your accomplishments. She would shake her head in amazement at how our garden has prospered. And blossomed.

"At this place in my life I am finally able to take that quest. I can choose any great ocean to sail, any passageway to explore. It would be an exciting expedition. I am free to wander.

"But along the way, a strange thing happened. You see, the MAN in me now cajoles me to take that trip. The man knows I deserve it, that all my responsibilities are finally fulfilled–that my dedication to family has borne fruit. The man says it is time. There is no longer a need to be the anchor.

Harry laughed, a joyous laugh. "But now it is the BOY who urges me to stay. He insists I still have that jaunty bounce in my step, that I can out-bat and out-field any of you, that I can dance in the rain. My youthful spirit sees an exciting journey still ahead on the horizon that exists right here," he waved his hand over the room, "a journey that crests even higher waves than the imaginary ones of my youth." He paused, then asked in a quiet voice, "Won't you join me, continuing this exhilarating ride? This time?"

Harry took the anchor pin and bent down to Susan. He fastened it on the young girl's shirt and kissed the top of her head. "Your journey is just beginning. Listen to your heart, my child," he whispered.

Then he raised his glass to his family, and proposed a toast. "To Love, to Honor and to Passion — the Rhythms of life."

Rhythm of the Soul

The second-floor children's ward at North Regional Children's Hospital was quiet when Dr. David Chen exited the elevator and started his rounds for the night shift. It was after 10:00 pm and of all his patients were apparently sound asleep in their beds. The only sounds heard were the beeping and buzzing of monitors taking vital signs.

Dr. Chen's patients were at different stages in their illnesses: many were undergoing chemotherapy or radiation for cancer. Some were struggling with stem cell transplants and others were battling an array of major illnesses. His heart ached with every step he took for what so many of his innocent patients and their families had to endure.

The doctor was a specialist in Oncology and Hematology. He had been treating children and adolescent patients for ten years. Yet for all his remarkable knowledge and education it was David Chen the person that the children related to. He made them feel comfortable enough to ask him questions about what to expect during their time in the hospital. They shared their discomforts, their worries, and their desires of being healthy and strong again. Over time, he felt he had seen it all, yet he still winced when they cried from a hurtful injection and held back tears watching them deal with the emotional and physical side effects of their treatments.

It was common practice not to become emotionally involved with a patient. Yet, when he conferred with parents and families about their loved ones, he felt their pain and what they were going through. He always spoke in terms of hope – even when the doctor in him knew better.

To see a depressed seven-year-old break into a smile from a silly joke he shared when David Chen approached, made his entire afternoon feel lighter. "Way to go!" he called out, clapping for the eleven-year-old girl who rose from her bed to sit up a day after surgery. David's heart went out to those who were afraid and suffering.

The children's oncology wing at North Regional Children's Hospital overlooked Main Street in their small Nebraska town of Harper Canyon. Downtown's daily happenings, great and small, were on display below, through a large wall-to-wall window that was in each child's room.

Colorful shops lined the streets, many with white awnings helping to shield the afternoon sun, each with its unique sign displayed — Coffee & Expresso, Fred's Barber Shop, Benny's Bakery – together with the all-enveloping delicious sweet smells from the bakery that wafted upwards into offices, buildings and even through the hospital windows. Honking cars, people calling out to each other, children and their parents eating ice cream cones filled the sidewalks below.

Across the street above the stores and restaurants were brick apartments, one building brown, the next yellow, then orange. Each apartment had its tiny balcony jutting out surrounded by a square black wrought iron fence. On nice days, the residents would sit on chairs, waving to friends, enjoying the sights and sounds of the Harper Canyon townspeople.

At nighttime, darkened skies became gilded with blinking lights and neon signs. Sometimes, a few of Dr. Chen's patients given to insomnia gathered at the window in the late hours, looking at the colorful lights below. Occasionally, on a night shift, Dr. Chen stood with them pointing upwards at a spattering of star clusters, or a brilliant half-moon. If they listened closely, musical sounds would emanate from various bars down the block, or a street soloist singing for his late supper from any light-night stragglers passing by.

Watching life go on through a glass window gave the children foresight, the doctor knew. It was a glimpse of a world they related to. And it was almost within reach.

"When I get out, I am going to buy chocolates, and a million donuts from Benny's Bakery," a young patient told him. Getting donuts from the bakery was invariably mentioned.

"They're waiting...won't be long, Josie," he smiled. "Will you save some for me?"

Besides visiting the bakery, there were additional favorites, such visiting as the bookstore and seeing a movie on a Saturday afternoon.

The doctor knew that many would not make it off the ward let alone out on Main Street. But, instead of despairing in those cases, he called upon faith to take a hand. He was a most enthusiastic audience no matter the subject, and he had spoken to his children on almost every subject under the sun. Perhaps the most consistent theme was what they would be doing when they would be strong again, healed and ready to take on the world.

"A want to be a baseball pitcher", twelve-year-old Jose announced.

"I am going to be a dancer in ballet class," seven-year-old Chloe whispered in his ear.

"I can't wait to be back swimming in our backyard pool," preteen Kevin Jones confided.

Their doctor saw clarity in their widening eyes when they spoke. He knew their visions of the other side of these walls were true and real. The bravery of these patients amazed him. Many of the children held back tears when their family visited, so as not to worry them. Some told untruths about how they felt. David Chen watched these brave hearts perform when he knew they experienced pain and weakness.

He wished he had their courage to overlook adversity and to go after their dreams.

If only he had a magic wand to sweep over each bed and take the illnesses away from them forever.

His wanted to see them strong and healthy on the other side of these walls.

When a call came the following day from Dr. Martin Blake, Director of Operations at a hospital in Honolulu, Hawaii, Dr. Chen was taken off-guard. He kept asking himself, "why me?"

as the renowned physician told him about a job opening for a lead Hospital Administrator-cum-researcher/physician. It turns out they had heard about Dr. Chen and had done a quiet background on him, after seeing amazing articles written about him in medical journals.

"We are looking for an expert in research and policies, overseeing oncology issues that would be presented," Dr. Blake said. "We think you would be perfect. Would you be interested in this position?"

Shocked silence. Dr. Chen could not find the words to respond. The job would start in sixty days, Dr. Blake continued without losing a beat. The position would be at a modern clinic close to the ocean. All he would have to do would be give notice. They would do the rest, including supplying a hospital-owned condo on the beach. The pay offered was far above what he was earning working at North Regional Children's. His life as he knew it, would change. He would be working with other physicians to identify and find a cure for these childhood disorders but would not be dealing directly with patients.

"Can I get back to you?" he finally managed to stutter.

"Of course," Dr. Blake responded. "But don't wait too long."

At first, David Chen dismissed the possibility of changing his life in this way. He was born and raised in Harper Canyon. He had met his wife Irene when he was working as an intern at another hospital outside the city. Irene taught fourth graders at a local elementary school. They married a year later.

As the months passed, their relationship became stagnant —- mundane, no enthusiasm, no real plans or talks about the possibility of starting a family or even of a sustainable future together. The couple went to counseling but with no success, ended up having an amicable divorce. It was the year 2000 when David moved back to Harper Canyon.

Over the years, David met other women and dated on and off for a while. He continued his schooling and even after he was hired at North Regional Children's, he was taking additional classes, advancing in his degree. Soon, he was asked to be the main Pediatric Oncologist at North Regional. His years of studies in the medical field, along with in-person practice, working with physicians and specialists, made him a perfect candidate for this new job.

David thought about the surprising offer. It was an opportunity that may not come again, he knew. "If I decline, will I ever know what living near the ocean would feel like?" How many times have I talked about the ocean and palm trees and Pacific Islands with my kids on the ward? I've dreamed of palm trees, the ocean and watching whales and dolphins my whole life."

David's world had always been in this small town he called home. In his college years he stayed for months with friends, in a crowded apartment complex. He never thought there was anything different. The honking of horns, people's voices talking, laughing, yelling for someone down the street was the norm. As he grew older, his friends scattered to continue their lives, moving away and working at new jobs. His two best friends were long gone: one settled on the West Coast, in the Santa Rosa area of California, another relocated after spending time visiting his grandparents in a village in Italy. Throughout the years David received photos and videos of a world unbeknownst to him. He was captivated by miles of sky, mountains, and the ocean waves rising and falling, then flattening on shore.

Now, this new world was no longer out of reach, but waiting for him to make his presence known so it could show off its beauty in full display.

David spent a restless night, wondering what to do. It was a major decision and he wished there was someone whom he could consult with and advise. There was not. This was a decision only David could make. It involved his work, and his future.

At 4:00 a.m. he accepted the offer in his mind. At 9:00 a.m. he formally accepted with a call to Dr. Blake. "I would be honored to work with you and your staff," he said. "Thank you for reaching out to me."

The following weeks he went about preparing and arranging for his move. And when the day came for him to leave, he said goodbye to the staff, who felt like family. "Good luck, Dr. Chen." "We will miss you." "Please keep in touch." Hugs and good wishes surrounded him, making him feel as though he was engulfed in a warm, protective shield.

Then, it was time to bid farewell to his patients. Dr. Chen decided to tell his patients the truth. "Just as you have your dreams of what you want to do, so do I," he explained. "I have an amazing opportunity and I am going to go for this dream. I am going to be working with other doctors to fight these diseases, to find answers and develop better treatments for those like you who are sick."

Questions came at him about where he was going, about the job and about where he would live. He spent time with each of his patients, then quietly left each room with mixed feelings — anticipation and a heavy heart.

Ten days later, settled into his new home, he began work at his new position. His job was all it was expected to be, important and challenging. The doctor conferred daily with medical experts in his field. Physicians called him from around the world for information on new upcoming procedures and scientific evidence-based treatments. In his personal life, he went on a few dates with women he met and over the months made friends, many of them physicians where he worked and their families.

As the months passed, he still made calls back to North Regional Children's Hospital in Nebraska to check on his patients. Was Juan Garcia healed enough to go home?" he asked the physician who took over his position on the children's floor. "And what was the latest on Chloe Spencer?" He wanted to know.

Dr. Chen spent his days in his office overlooking the ocean. Evenings found him stretched out on his green beach chair outside his townhome, watching the sun disappear into hovering streaks of clouds in every color imaginable. Each sunset was different, but the movement was the same. The day's yellow glow inched downward, muting into the day's colorful clouds as the minutes passed. The doctor sat quietly his bare feet dug into the sand. Except for the song of sea-birds overhead there was no other noise around him.

"This is what heaven must feel like," he sighed. A tropical paradise. It was the music of waves, a painted sky and palm trees rustling nearby. Leaning his head back, he closed his eyes.

A vision appeared and startled him for a moment. He was back in North Regional Children's Hospital, tapping on a door of a patient's room. Slowly he paced over to the bed of his patient, a beautiful six-year-old girl named Emily. He checked the bags, tubes, and monitors at her bedside. He knew she should be outside of the walls, laughing, singing, interacting with her family and friends without a care in the world. But her movements inside were dictated. She had no choice. Dr. Chen and his medical staff were working around the clock to cure her, to alleviate her pain, to give her back her strength.

All he could do was try to quiet her fears. He was an expert at bringing forth a smile. He looked at her and made a silly face.

"You're funny," the young girl giggled. She made a face back to him.

David read her chart and knew what she was facing. He reached out to hold her hand and dropped down on one knee as he did with so many other young patients, so he would be face-to- face with her when they spoke. "No, you are funny," he told her, which brought forth a sweet laugh.

The scene faded with the amplifying sounds of seagulls overtaking the moment. David blinked twice and opened his eyes. His hand unconsciously wiped his brow. These visions were happening more and more. Sometimes they appeared when he was sitting quietly at a long table in the conference

Page | 181

room with other physicians. Or in the middle of listening to a pediatric neurologist talk about an exciting new trial that was being worked on. Or at his workstation in the lab late at night one would appear. It felt so real, it was if he had been transported back to his job at North Regional.

Nevertheless, in his present world, however, the vast beauty that surrounded him did not disappoint. He had made friends. Over the months he had gone on several dates in the bustling downtown area. With a sweet lady at his side, they visited art museums, Botanical Gardens and ate at picturesque oceanfront restaurants.

But even during these times, the past was not fully erased. It insinuated itself constantly. Sometimes when he least expected it, he recalled sweet moments with his patients: especially eleven-year-old Jason, talking with him about baseball. Jason played on a neighborhood team. He shared his excitement with his doctor about batting the ball out of the park, running at super speed to make it to base, catching someone's pop-up to prevent a home run, which won the game. Dr. Chen listened to the children as a friend. He made comments that made the young boy laugh, his eyes clear and alert as he spoke.

During those times, David Chen felt fully immersed in a place that medicines could not reach. Soon, the staff would be at work again giving the pills, injections and x-rays that would work towards recovery. But the personal time spent with his patients, side-by-side in their lives – totally hooked into their feelings and thoughts — was assuring. It was where he was supposed to be: using his knowledge and his heart, helping others to heal.

It wasn't just the patient connections that were tugging at him lately. It was the memories of his Nebraska town. He had been in Hawaii almost two years, yet he still thought about summer thunderstorms. He recalled breathtaking rows of autumn trees that lined the neighborhoods.

He remembered Halloween in October, where farmers lined up haystack squares displaying carved pumpkins faces staring at the cars driving by. The aromas coming from expresso shops, the mixture of voices, young and old from the townspeople, all of them the various memories of small-town life. He did not have to try hard to be happy there. Contentment was his friend.

He had been too close to it to see it when he walked away. At that time, the appreciation of all that was quirky and familiar took a back seat and could not compete with the amazing new life he was embarking on.

Just recently, David heard that one of the specialists at North Regional had left and they were looking for someone to replace him. His thoughts drifted. He knew he could stay on in Hawaii, working in his current position. He already was offered a substantial raise if he would sign on for another year.

David could be set in his job and make a beautiful life for himself in this magnificent area of the world. Yet, his mind would not let him be. It reminded him constantly, of the place where he had lifelong friends, where he found work and showed up daily at a job he loved. But there was an emotional pull that he had been fighting. He realized what place his heart was truly connected to.

Now—

Back in Nebraska, the 4th of July Harper Canyon parade crept slowly down the street with Sheriff Martin as Grand Master. He stood up in the old model Lincoln driven by his deputy, waving, bowing, greeting people on each side as the marching band boomed. The crowds cheered each decorated float that inched by. The sound of drums and clarinets punctuated the loud whistles and clapping of the crowds. Sheriff Martin's car slowed right under the windows of the Children's floor at North Regional. Boys and girls were lined up at the windows in their rooms, looking down at the spectacular parade.

"Stop right here," the Sheriff bellowed. He held his hand up for the cars and floats to turn off their engines directly below the hospital windows. Sheriff Martin looked up and tipped his hat to each child. He clapped and saluted them, and they waved back. From one end to the other, each responded. Loud applause erupted from those on the floats, the band and from the deputy at the wheel. The cheers were met with smiles and sounds of laughter down the hallway from each of the hospital rooms on the floor

---

A group of children at the window tugged at the white coat of the doctor standing next to them He was smiling as well, and saluted back to the Sheriff whom he recognized.

The young ones laughed, pointing to the floats and the marching bands below. He turned to his patients and slowly his eyes filled. A tear ran down his face.

"Are you sad?" a young boy asked.

"No, I am happy," he told him.

"Then I am happy!" the boy grinned, hugging him.

David Chen blinked twice to see clearly the emotional scene before him. Was this another vision? He wondered. They had always felt so real.

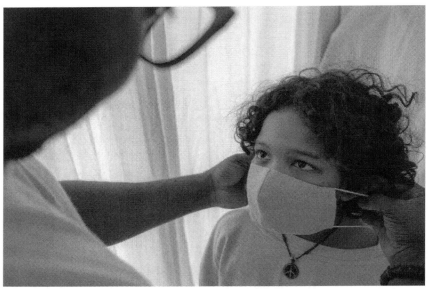

But he was not looking out at palm trees. There was no ocean water merging in the distance to a lowering sun. At this moment, he was chatting with patients, and hearing clearly the joyful sounds below. The music started up and the parade proceeded down Main Street.

This was not his imagination. He knew that he was truly back and what was happening before him was in real-time. He could close his eyes and open them, and his surroundings were unwavering.

David Chen realized that while there is a calmness in the rhythm of the sea, there is also a rhythm of the soul. It is a connection that brings forth fond memories and joy. Not unlike the tranquil sound of ocean waves hitting shore, rhythm of the soul nurtures. It holds dear all that is familiar. It comes from within, connecting with the heart in a tempo of its own, embracing goodness and wonder.

The doctor knew his soul was connected, for he felt peace. He felt comfort.

He was home.

"My soul is full of longing for the secret of the sea,

and the heart of the great ocean
sends a thrilling pulse through me."

—Henry Wadsworth Longfellow

Author's Note

For as long as I can remember, I have loved being near the water. From my earlier days growing up in Minnesota, it was weekends spent with my family on Lake Minnetonka that were fun and relaxing. Now, it is near the shore of the Pacific Coast that I find peaceful and exciting. It is not always the sunny, perfect days by the water that is most gratifying but the stormy ones as well...thunder and lightning, coastal mist and fog. Being attuned to the rhythm of the waters generated the original book and continued writing of this collection of short stories. I hope you connect with some of them and that they bring inspiration and thought to your own lives.

With new challenging times we are experiencing throughout the world, I continue to write. I find myself going deeper into my imagination when creating new stories that I am hoping will resonate with others. These stories continue to be related to the sea- to the waters around us. I am hoping they will bring a sense of peace and calmness to the soul.

It is our children's children that now appear on the cover of my expanded book *Rhythm of the Sea*. I view them as not just the new generation, but as unique individuals who have their own thoughts and feelings about what they are experiencing in the moment. I wonder about their future. Will they love the sea as I do? Or will they form a life- connection to endless miles of deserts or vast mountain ranges? Time will tell. I will understand, wherever their hearts lead them.

Thank you, Dr. Bud Banis of Science and Humanities Press for taking notice of my book Rhythm of the Sea several years ago and now, offering once again a place for my expanded book of stories to appear on your BeachHouse Books list. From our first correspondence I felt we had an immediate connection to the subject matter.

I am grateful to Dr. Jeff Conine, author, writing professor and editor for the guidance he has helped me with over the years, bringing light to my stories.

A heartfelt thank you to my husband Paul for your continued support- always having available the time and space I need to create my stories. Love to my family, our children, their spouses and our adored four grandchildren.

This book is dedicated to the memory of my Dad Irv. He was a gentle man who enjoyed fishing and loved to spend his leisure hours on and near the water.

Dear Readers, if you would like to share your own "Rhythm of the Sea" stories or have comments about the book, please write me through my email at www.sharicohen.com

or at P. O. Box 6826 Malibu, CA 90264

Shari

Made in the USA
Columbia, SC
12 October 2021